HUNGER

Tanzeela K. Hassan

THAZBOOK PUBLICATIONS

HUNGER
Copyright © 2020 by THAZBOOK

This book is a work of fiction. Names, characters, businesses, organizations, places, events and incidents either are the product of the author's imagination or are used fictitiously. Any resemblance to actual persons, living or dead, events, or locales is entirely coincidental.

For information contact :
Thazbook
03333299920
E-128 BLOCK-6 PECHS, KARACHI.
www.facebook.com/thazbook1
http://www.thazbook.com

Book and Cover design by Thazbook Designs.
ISBN: 978-969-7851-12-6
This Edition: march 2020

To My Husband.

1

LIKE THE fire that doesn't care if it burns the wood or the flesh, Max had no preferences at all. In his world, he only cared about giving them what they deserved rather than what they desired.

That night turned out to be the perfect one, for Max finally achieved everything he had longed for. He glared at the restrained, bearded man and his terrified wife. A smile playing on his lips as the shaft of his dagger cooled his clammy palm, with a graceful dance the blade sliced through the thick air. Hatred burned in his heart so deep, that it ingrained in every tissue of his body. The man with the beard rocked against the chair, pulling and twisting, trying to wrench himself free. The duct tape gag barely muted his screams.

The fool. There was nothing he could do now.

Not only the husband but the wife twisted and pulled, the heavy oak bed moved with her as she tried to free herself, praying and pleading, which Max couldn't understand. He was about to give her the freedom she deserved; to let her free her soul from the burdens of the world and her unborn too, for he knew that it was never a possibility to give any child a safe and prosperous existence. Indeed, he felt it his duty to keep her from bringing healthy and happy offspring into the world, only to turn them into filthy and wanton beings.

Max had never listened to them — never had, never would. He tightened his chest and placed the sharp edge of the curved blade over her shivering throat. *A massacre dripped from the walls, collecting in pools of sticky crimson on the polished wooden floor.*

ADAM COULD feel the heat. Strong and furious. Never had a desert — dry, hot, and sandy — surrounded him. He could not see much farther than the winding dunes of sand. There was nothing but the smouldering sun. He gulped and tried to moisten his tongue. His saliva became thicker like wallpaper paste, as if his body refused to produce it. He scrambled towards the sun to look for a way out. There was no end to it — just dry, hot sand everywhere.

Suddenly, he saw a hut, a small bright structure right in front of him. A soft, long lost smile cracked his face. Nothing that felt this perfect could be wrong. It just couldn't. He wasn't feeling tired or thirsty anymore — the mere sight of the hut made him energetic and strong.

He walked to the door of the small wooden hut, painted white, with engraved flowers. The doorknob

— a big round flower. A daisy. It creaked open before he could even reach it. A fresh breeze came from inside, and he smelled the pleasant scent.

He found it empty, except for a table in the centre of the room. The walls were bare and there were no windows. He moved towards the table, almost as if an invisible force pulled him in its direction. On the table was a book — out of which a bright light shone out, a light so strong that it blinded him, calling him, daring him to touch. He reached towards it...

...and...

Something slimy and sticky blocked his view. He struggled to get rid of it and brushed his hands over his face. It oozed over his eyes and mouth, crawling into his pores. He opened his eyes and saw Wild licking his face off. Shivering and all wet with sweat, Adam found himself on his bed. Bright sunlight streamed in through the large windows in his room. Although the sun was barely above the horizon, yet it could peek through the windows of his penthouse. He stayed still for a few minutes, musing on the dream.

"That was only a dream, Wild." Adam patted his dog, "and I'll be late if I don't get up," he said while getting out of the bed and glancing at his watch. It was past seven o'clock in the morning, and he had a nine o'clock meeting with his lawyer; the purpose of which he could not understand.

"Meet me tomorrow at my office. It's urgent," the lawyer had said the day before.

"What's the urgency, Mark? I don't seem to have any legal issues. Or do I, that I don't know of yet?" He inquired.

"Well, look, Adam. It's complicated! I can't tell you on the phone. I have to meet you in person."

The lawyer, his childhood friend, Mark Evince — the son of his father's friend, and his family lawyer Evince Anderson, the only person in this world whom his father trusted. Adam's father, David, had worked from his home. Being a single parent, he had to run the company and take care of his only son all at the same time. David had always been busy making money. His mother, well, he had never seen her in his life. How could he — she died before Adam took his first breath. He always wondered what his mother would be like and how life would have been with her around, caring for him, listening to his stories, giving him a shoulder to cry on. Then after his father left him alone, he had stopped thinking about them and engrossed himself in his own life, leaving the relations behind. Working for himself. Living for himself.

"Here you go."

Adam gave Wild his breakfast and walked towards the door. The dog yelped and munched. As soon as he opened the door, right in front of him, stood the girl who called herself Anna. She lived one storey below, always coming by, willing to provide help, letting herself in, and making his life a lot more vexatious.

"Hi, I've brought fresh homemade waffles. I gathered you'd like'em," Anna said.

Exasperated, he took the platter and without saying a word, he slammed the door in her face. Tossing it into the bin, he turned and let his eyes slide across the reflection of his cold, uncaring self.

O N THE other side of the east river, not far from Adam, yet living in an entirely different world, Iman opened her eyes with the memories of the night before.

She had been sitting at the dining table for hours, satisfied with her day's work, all set and settled. She had made the most exquisite dinner that day, For only one other person – Ahmed Ghani, the person she had given her heart to, and the person around whom her life revolved.

Oh, it's eleven o'clock now, Iman had thought. Where is he? I told him we will celebrate our first anniversary together. Why is he being so difficult? Maybe I should call him.

After listening to the recorded message of his phone being switched off, she threw her mobile away, bent her head and crossed her hands around it.

At midnight she heard the front door of her small apartment slammed hard.

"Assalamualaikum, let me take this," she said, with a smile on her face.

"Wàlikumassallam." With that, he walked past her and went to the rest room without even glancing at her, though she had spent hours to get ready for the night.

"Oh, please help me," she said, looking up and raising her hands.

"Ahmed, are you all right? I've been waiting for you," she said the moment he came out.

"And why was that?" Ahmed answered in a monotone.

"Remember, I told you it's our anniversary. I've made us a royal dinner. Please, have some?"

"What? Oh, our anniversary. Sorry. I forgot, and I had my dinner at the office. I'm so tired. I think I'd better go to bed now."

"But — Ah," Iman sighed as he left her alone in the living area.

SO, WHAT'S the big deal Mark, eh?" asked Adam as he walked into the lawyer's office, his hands stuffed in his pockets. He couldn't help glancing over the fresh renovation: a highly polished wooden desk and elaborated wall hangings.

Mark started, "Calm down, Adam." He pointed toward a mahogany armchair in front of him, "First, take a seat, and tell me how's life?"

"You called an urgent meeting to know how my life is?"

"I'm just being nice."

"If you please, tell me what this is all about?"

"Where should I start?" Mark said and leaned back, tapping a pen against his chin. "It's about your grandmother, your maternal one. She is alive, and she contacted dad's office for you," said Mark.

"What did you say?" Adam went on when his mind finally processed what he had heard. "My mother's mother — you mean, my grandmother — she's alive?" Adam brought a palm to his face and rubbed his eyes, chuckling as he shook his head. "Nice joke."

"It's not a joke, Adam. I think you should take this seriously," Mark said, leaning forward in his chair and fumbling for something on his unkempt desk. He pulled out an envelope from under a stack of papers and extended his arm for Adam to take it. "She lives in Pakistan. Here's her letter for you. She says she wants to meet you."

"Let me get this straight," Adam narrowed his eyes in disbelief, then continued, "She's my grandmother, yet how come I'm the only one not informed about this? And your father should've known. Why didn't he tell me anything about her before?"

Mark sighed, tossed the letter onto his desk, leaned back, crossed his arms and said, "I don't know. I would ask him if I could, but you know his condition. He's been in a coma for like, what, about a year now?"

"Yes, I know."

"But, I have something that will at least answer some of your questions." Mark turned to the bookshelves behind him and picked up a small brown box.

"What's this?"

"It's all I could find in dad's office about you and your family. You can take it home."

"Thanks," said Adam.

He took the box and his grandmother's letter and went straight home.

5

FOR OVER two decades Max's nostrils had been taking in the stench that made its way through the large window of his cell. He had been to three prisons until he finally took a halt at this one, which was different. At first, the large spacious cell felt pleasant with the iron bar window and natural light coming in. However, the mere fact that the cell had no means of personal sanitation and almost all the prisoners threw their litter out through their windows, was enough to remind him of his sentence for twenty-five years; a good part of his life. After everything he had done for this world, after all he had been doing to give them what was best, they had only given him the worst, and they had always been this way. All of them: his father and his father's father and his friends and his friends' friends. They had always made him walk on thorns.

"You bastard, I told you to throw this away, and you didn't

listen?" Father grabbed him by his short curls and dragged him out of their small apartment's door. Pointing towards the bag of trash he said, "Pick it up and throw it into the bin."

"Which bin, we don't have one."

"You coward."

Max only remembered the spanks and kicks after that and so many other times when he refused to do things that his father wanted him to do. Things such as throwing their trash in front of the neighbour's door and leaving their dog's litter across the street were fresh in his memories.

DEAR GRANDSON *Adam, How are you? I hope you are well. I wonder what you look like and how much you have of your mother. I learned about your father's death a few months ago, and since then I have been trying very hard to get to you. Your father disconnected all available modes of communication from me after your mother left this world. He took you, returned to America and never contacted me again. I tried to get ahold of him often, but he would not even speak over the phone. I do not blame him at all, for life sometimes provides such hardships one cannot bear.*

It is awkward of me to ask, but you are the only family I have left now. I am over eighty years old, and I lastly hope to meet you, kiss you, and tell you about your mother, which I'm sure you would love to hear.

I have lived in Scotland all of my married life; now I am back to my native country, Pakistan, in the house of our ancestors, and I will live here till my death. It is a small village in Gilgit, Baltistan. Also, my health does not allow me to travel much.

Please, my dear grandson, come and visit me. I have many of your mother's memories, and I cannot wait to share them with you.

I am attaching my address and a travel guide's number along with some details. He will guide you to my place.

Waiting for you.

Hugs and kisses

Your grandmother,

Mamma.

A strong wave of uncertainty rushed through Adam's blood — throwing the letter straight into the bin, he sat back on his couch and placed both of his hands over his face. He could hear the damp morning air hitting the thick glass and the muffling sounds of his dog's musings. He turned his face towards Wild and said, "There must be a reason why father cut her off. Could a sensible man like dad do such a thing?" He asked. Wild wagged his tail in affirmative.

"I'm not going anywhere, not at all—travelling across the oceans to meet her, just because that's what she wants... Besides, I need to work on the project I badly wanted to do. I am not even sure if she really is my grandmother," he said, and within seconds contradicted his own thoughts, "What if she is? What if she knows things I have missed in my life?" he said and peeked inside the box he had received from Mark's office. There were several papers cluttered within; his father's will, his business papers, some photographs...

... And letters.

He instantly recognised them. The handwriting on the letters was exactly the same as the one he had received from Mark — the letter he had just read. There were a lot, at least fifty. Some were old, while others were relatively new — all of them short and precise, and written with the same request:

Let me see my grandson.

IMAN'S MORNING had begun with an unusual occurrence. She found an empty bed.

"I should call him and ask why he didn't wake me up." She picked up the phone and found a note under it.

I'm heading to the office. Have a meeting at seven. Please don't call.

After finishing her daily chores she packed herself a lunch and ambled down to the Indian grocery market, the place that always made her feel better. Every time she saw those Pakistanis and Indians, she would find herself deep in the memories of her homeland. She would walk past the neighbourhood and feel the surrounding atmosphere. The people talking in Urdu, the smell of pickles, and the fights among the kids felt like heaven.

Walking by the block just round the corner of her street, she stopped for a moment to take in the smell of Nihari and fresh Naan. Her face broke into a smile which soon faded away as her mind started wandering to her life back in her homeland. She looked up to the signboard that said, The Taste Of Lahore, smiled again, and started crossing the road.

"Are you going towards the Masjid Khazra as well?" asked an old lady, wearing a white Shilwar Khameez, "We can walk together if you'd like."

"Isn't it at least twenty-minutes walk from here?"

"Yes, it is. But I enjoy long walks, besides, what else should I do?"

Iman smiled and said, "I would love to walk with you."

They turned their attention towards the street and saw heavy traffic ahead. The lady said, "Lets take the other street; I don't want to get stuck in the high school traffic."

"Sure."

"So Baita, what are your worries? I can see that you have many," asked the old lady when they reached the bench near the Hospital.

"Not much. I sometimes feel lonely here."

"Don't you have a family? Kids?"

"It's been only nine months since I've moved here from Pakistan. I live with my husband, and his family's down South."

"Ah, then make friends. There are lots of Pakistanis, plus Indians who could be great friends to you."

"I don't know. Maybe someday I will," she sighed.

"Your husband, what does he do? Doesn't he spare time for you?"

"Well, he's a busy man. I don't really know much of his job, but he goes out early and comes home late."

"Oh, then you should find friends. Living alone like this is not good for your health."

"Will you be my friend?"

"Sure Baita, I come here every morning for a walk, so you could join me. Here, keep my number. You can call me whenever you need." She produced a small pad and a pen from her bag, wrote her number on a page, and handed it over to Iman.

"Thank you. I think I should go now. I'll meet you tomorrow maybe. The Masjid isn't far from here. I hope walking alone won't be an issue?"

"Sure, baita. I can walk. I walk down this path all the time. Take care, and do call me."

Iman said farewell and walked towards the path to her apartment. As if her sixth sense called, she followed it to her door, and saw his car. She immediately knew that her sixth sense's call was not just out of thin air. Something was wrong. For the first time, he had come home early.

8

THE FOURTH room of the A-wing had an unfamiliar yet pleasant smell of the air freshener and wax that the cleaning staff had used for that particular day. Max sat there on the third iron chair among the other prisoners, waiting for his turn, nervously tapping over the scar on the right side of his face.

"Maxwell, you're next. Get up and follow me."

He stood up and followed the man with a gruesome look over his face and a prison guard's uniform over his round belly.

9

THE ROOM adjacent to the fourth room of the A-wing had nothing but a small white desk and two chairs, yet, unlike the rest of the prison, it was filled with the smell of the exact same air freshener and wax. Maxwell took his place opposite the very man he had been meeting once a month for the past twenty-two years of his life.

"Do you remember for how many years you have been here with us?" said the counsellor, fumbling some pages of the grey file.

"Yes, I do."

He looked up tilting his reading glasses sideways and said, "Three years. And you do know that if you behave well and work hard, you could be released in two or even fewer?"

"Yes, I do."

"What have you learned in the past month?" said

the counsellor.

"I have been reading a lot."

"Great! What kind of books?"

"General books."

"Any specific genre?"

"Mystery and suspense."

"Try reading self-help books, you'll love them for sure."

"If you say so," he replied with a soft smile.

"What about making friends here? Have you tried talking to the new guy? I think he is your type."

"I have, but he seems a little off track."

"What do you mean by off track?"

"I mean he is disturbed. He never answers or talks to anyone. He just sits in the corner watching everyone else."

"It's Normal. Remember how quiet you were when you first came here? You should try anyway."

"Yes, I will try to talk to him for sure."

"Great. I must remind you that if you wish to be free this year you have to stay away from trouble, far away from rocky and his party. I hope you understand the fact that my hands are tied by whatever you do in prison." The counsellor closed the file and looked straight into his eyes.

"Yes, I do."

10

GOLDEN BEAMS of sunlight pierced through the large windows of Adam's living room, filling the surrounding space along with the smell of the pre-cooked food he had a while ago. The penthouse being on top of a huge building in Manhattan presented a perfect picture, straight from a catalogue. He had bought it from his father when his construction business was in full bloom. It wasn't easy for Adam to buy such a place with his not-so-big salary, but he wouldn't take a single penny from his father.

"Son, everything I do is for you. It's yours already, so why don't you go live there?" David would often say whenever Adam mentioned that he wanted to buy the penthouse.

Adam's thigh vibrated. He picked his phone which was blinking with Sidney's name. "Oh, crap! I had a four o'clock meeting with the director."

"Hey, Sidney! Tell me you cancelled my meeting

today 'cause I'm not at all in a mood to attend it."

"No, that's not at all possible. You should work with your mood problems. This project can't be delayed. It's as important for your career as it is for our firm," she answered.

"Don't order me like this. I don't like this happy-caring attitude of yours. I will be there. Don't tell everybody about my absence this morning," he said and tossed his phone on the couch.

THOUGH IT was a daily venture for Adam to cross Central Park all the way to Columbus Circle, that day the air felt different. Everything was beautiful—even the pond looked more enchanting than before. He didn't understand what exactly had happened to him. People were talking here and there.

"I wonder what my grandma looks like." The moment he uttered those words, he was devastated. Why couldn't he take these thoughts out of his head? Why hadn't his father said anything about her before? It could have slipped from his mouth anytime. How could he erase one of the most important members of our family. The more he thought about it, the more he became confused. Anger and hatred grew stronger.

Then he noticed something — an old woman and a young man, playing like kids, tickling. He could hear them talk; the man was busy telling stories about his life, with "Grandma" this and "Grandma" that.

Adam stood there for a whole minute just to watch them. They looked happy, complete, and divine. There is nothing better than being with loved ones. Her grandson carried her to a wheelchair, and they moved ahead, right towards Adam, who started walking again the moment he realised they were watching him.

What was the matter with him? Where did his sense of reason go? He would not typically glance at anyone. It was not in his wheelhouse. He would never act like this. Yet, it felt pleasant; he enjoyed the scene.

12

"GO STRAIGHT to Tom's office. He's waiting for you," Sidney said as soon as Adam arrived at his office.

"Wait — He's waiting already? It's not even four o'clock. I'm not at all late here."

"Correct. You're not late, but somebody told him you didn't come in the morning, so he's angry about it."

"That somebody better not be you. Besides, it's my first time. That's insane."

"It's what people call a boss — insane and exactly the one you are being here."

"You know you're unbelievable," he said as he left.

“WHAT’S YOUR problem? You’re acting irresponsible these days. Your project’s proposal is still pending, yet, you took a leave this morning? You should have been here to complete it,” said Tom Braiden. The moment Adam entered his office, he picked up on the smell of lavender.

“You know, most bosses would ask, ‘How’s life?’ Or ‘are you feeling better?’ when their employee takes a leave after a long time,” Adam said.

“Let’s say, I’m not the kind,” Tom replied. “Look, here’s the deal. I want your project’s proposal ready to present it to the client by the end of this day. We’ve arranged a dinner meeting with the client to calm them down; the least they can ask is a nice proposal today. Do it for me, or leave the project.”

“What? Today? That’s ridiculous! You know it was only the day before yesterday I started working on this project. These things take time. How could you arrange a meeting before even telling me?"

"You're not the President of the United States of America. Besides, the client's been waiting for the proposal for about a week now. We can't just tell them we had some problems with the architects here. The meeting is tonight. Head back to your office and work on it."

14

WANTING TO concentrate on the project, he sat in his office. It was a small room with everything he needed at his disposal, yet, with a clean look; only the balls of crushed drawing sheets scattered the floor as he tried again and again to work on it. His emotions were exceptional for he had never felt disturbed or distracted towards his work, the purpose of his life.

"I need coffee," he said to Sidney, holding the receiver between his head and shoulder.

"You need another coffee, would be more appropriate," she said.

"Whatever. I need it hot, so get up now," he said while putting the receiver back. He bent down to the desk and tried to relax.

"What are you doing? Your meeting with the client is still on schedule. You know that right?" Adam looked up, holding a cup of coffee in one hand and the papers in the other, Sidney glared straight at him.

"How did you do that? Adam inquired. "You can't just fly downstairs to get me a cup of coffee."

"I was already on my way back. I knew it was time for your refill before you could even order," she said after placing the cup on his desk.

"Do you have any suggestions about how I can get rid of the meeting tonight? I can't just go there with no proposal." Adam cursed himself the minute he said those words.

Since when did you allow yourself to ask help from others? He asked himself furiously as he got up from his desk and headed towards the exit. His mind was blank.

Just blank.

He didn't have a clue what he was doing or where he was going. He walked and walked. Lost in his thoughts. The simple question was killing him.

Why?

Why would his father do such a thing? Why didn't he tell him anything about his mother? He remembered a time when he thought maybe his father had adopted him, or worse, they did not get married at all.

"Dad, please tell me something about your family... my family. There must be something you're hiding." He remembered asking questions that day while fishing at the lake by their home. Those were his golden days.

He could never forget those moments with his father: trying to catch fish, waiting for them, talking about different things, mostly sports. They would sit there for hours. But never did his father answer any of his inquiries about his mother or their past. That day, he insisted his father tell him the truth. He was almost fifteen years old then; it was time for him to know the truth of his past, but his father ended the fishing expedition and shut himself up to his room.

"I won't ask him anything more about it. Maybe it's meant to be that I am better off without the truth," he said to himself that night, after he had settled things with his father.

"Please, sir. I am needy. A dollar won't change your life, but it will do wonders in mine," said a man in tattered clothes.

Adam returned from his train of thoughts and tried to make sense out of the man's words. Yes, a few things are worthless for some and worthwhile for others. He didn't know what came over him. He took his wallet out, handed the ragged man a ten-dollar bill, and marched away.

Sitting on a bench across the park, lost deep in thoughts, he searched his pockets for the planner that his father had always kept with him and never showed it to anyone; even Adam was not allowed to touch it but ever since his father died, almost for the past two years, Adam had kept it in his pocket. He tried to find out the reason for the secrecy, yet he couldn't. To him it was just an ordinary planner that contained his father's daily schedule, personal account records, and a few event details — nothing else. Although Adam couldn't find a purpose in keeping it, he couldn't bring himself to get rid of it. Reading it, again and again, became a habit. To know that there was somebody dear to him, to whom he was the dearest, was the thought that could make his day. Whenever he felt frustrated or angry at his life, he would read it and his anger would flush away. Unlike any other day, he did not feel fulfilled, even after reading pages and pages of it. There was something festering in his mind.

"Where are you right now?" his boss inquired, as he answered his ringing phone. Adam looked at his watch — it was past six o'clock in the evening, almost dark. He was sitting on the bench alone, and all the people at the park had gone, vanished.

Adam cleared his throat. "In the park."

"In the park? What are you doing there? I thought I told you to finish the proposal before seven."

"I'm sorry. I can't do it today," Adam said, blankly.

"A sorry doesn't fix my day, and I'm not accepting it. Not from you. And you know what? You keep that attitude of yours and leave my firm. I don't want anyone who's this irresponsible. No — I can't handle your kind. Please pick up your things tomorrow," Tom said.

"How could you? This was one time, first time I

haven't been able to do my work, and you're acting as if I'm always like this," he retorted and sat up straight.

"Don't tell me what I can and what I can't do. You knew how important this project was to me and my firm, yet you acted like this? First time my foot, it's your last time..."

The line went dead before he could even hear the complete sentence. Boiling with furious thoughts, Adam threw his phone to the bench and covered his face with both his hands.

"WHERE DID you go? Shouldn't you be at home? Don't you have your chores?" Ahmed bashed a series of inquiries as Iman entered the house. There in the middle of the coffee table she saw Ahmed's travel bag.

"I went for a walk," Iman mumbled the answer.

"A walk? Don't you have any little sense? Can't you see for yourself? I don't really know what came over me when I married you; you're the most stupid girl I have ever met. Go pack your stuff; we are leaving."

"Leaving? Where?"

"Will you ever listen without being irritating for once?"

"What do you want me to pack, and for how many days?"

"I don't know, just pack the necessary things... your visa and other papers, and also, all the jewellery you have," he peeked through the thick curtains. Iman stood there dumbstruck by his behaviour.

"What? Why are you not moving? Hurry girl, we don't have all day. They could be here any minute."

Iman rushed inside, deeply lost in her own thoughts. She opened her drawer, produced her passport, wrapped it in a zip-lock bag along with the bag of her jewellery, and placed them together inside a big plastic bag. Leaving it on her bed, she ran back to the cupboard but the moment she took her small carry-on out of her cupboard, she heard something smashing. In seconds Ahmed rushed inside, his bag swinging over his elbow. Within an instant, he grabbed her arm while picking up the zip-lock bag; he dragged her out of their apartment using the fire escape.

"Just run! We need to move fast," Ahmed said, while climbing down the ladder. He shifted his bag over his shoulder and jumped down the last bar. They ran as fast as they could, crossed the market and headed towards the subway station. Iman looked back and saw three huge, white men. They were nothing but some gangsters, exactly the kind she had seen in the movies; black leather jackets with little French beards and bald heads. She could feel their big steps behind them. When they reached the mouth of the staircase that would lead them to the subway station, Ahmed took a sharp turn down a narrow alley and dashed inside through the coffee shop's back door. The bald-headed men stopped at the door. One of them took his place near the back door, and others waited outside the front.

"Sit." Ahmed took his place at the empty bar. He glanced at the front to find the two of them staring right through the big glass window.

"Want anything?" the bartender inquired in a dull voice. Catching his breath, Ahmed shook his head, and she returned to her work without a hitch.

"Are you honestly going to tell me what's going on?" Iman finally found the courage to ask.

"It's a long story. I owe something to my boss and now he has sent these men to get it."

"Why don't you give them what they want and leave this stupid company? Who in their right mind would hire such men?"

"I wish it could be that easy. I don't have it with me," Ahmed replied, turning around to glance at the door.

"What do you mean you don't have it?"

"Ah, you're such an annoying person. I said I owe them, that doesn't mean I still have it. Oh, leave it. Here is the drill; you need to go back home, pack your stuff and leave. I have booked a flight for you next Thursday morning. Stay away and stay safe until then." Ahmed reached into his pocket, produced a PIA ticket and placed it over her passport.

"What do you mean? Is this a ticket to Pakistan?

Are you not going with me? These men are waiting for us. How do you think we can ditch them?"

"Girl! They are waiting for me, not you; if only you hadn't gone, we could've been far away from them. I know I have no choice but to surrender, yet I need you to go back home. I have messed with you a lot."

"Why? Who are these people? We could go to the police, you know."

"No — we can't, they won't believe me and the next thing we know, I would end up in jail. Besides, I need to set the record straight; I need to talk to him. You must go. I'll be fine. I'm used to it."

"I don't get it. Why aren't they coming in? It's only a coffee shop." Iman looked back to the window; two of them were still standing right by the door.

"Ah! Them," Ahmed said pointing towards two men sitting by the door, dressed in civilian clothes, "they are the off-shift police officers; there is a police station across the street. I came here because I knew there would be at least a few of them."

The moment Ahmed said those words an officer in a blue uniform came near and stared right at them.

"Are you Mr Ahmed and Mrs Ahmed?"

"*Yes.*"

"*No.*"

"You both need to come with me."

"Is there any problem, Sir? There must be a

misunderstanding I am an upstanding citizen," Ahmed said, as he stood up.

"We'll see if you are, for now, please come," the officer said and walked to the front door. A different walk, casual yet calculated. They both looked at each other, and Ahmed signalled for her to walk beside him. At least the guy is an officer; everything will be fine, Iman thought and followed Ahmed, walking closely. The officer showed them to a black unmarked car.

"Please get in."

"It's fishy; these uniformed officers usually have marked cars. Besides, who would want a car only to cross the street?" Ahmed whispered, while getting in. His mind was working fast, but not fast enough. Within seconds, two of the huge guys settled themselves in, squeezing Ahmed and Iman in between; the third one took the passenger seat, and the officer took the driver's seat and hit the gas as fast as he could. Before Ahmed could protest anything, they were off on the road towards downtown.

16

ADAM PLACED the box on the coffee table; the little dying beams of sunlight pierced through the open curtains and blinding him. Picking up the remote, he pressed the close button.

Serves me right for not opening my own firm, I could've started it ages ago. Adam thought while moving the soft cushion under his head. He laid down on the couch and closed his eyes, only to bring back the memories of the dream, the book, and the hut.

"I have to finish it before it finishes me. I have to find the answer to the why. It's eating me and I will not let it," he said to himself, feeling invigorated, as if suddenly he had found the solution to his emptiness.

17

THE NEW prisoner had a pale face with dark-circled, blue eyes and blond hair. He was of the age where a man begins to acknowledge his actions, exactly the age at which they had brought in Max, twenty-two years back. The guy showed a light smile trying to hide his anxiety when Max first reached him.

"Hi, I am Max, and you?"

"I am Dexter..." Max could see his terrified eyes fixed on his scar. The scar he had got from his best friend.

"I gather you're here for a life sentence too? I was here for two but mine's ending in three years." Max patted his shoulder.

"Yes, one."

"What did you do?"

"Killed my father."

"I've put mine to rest too, but they never found out it was me," Max whispered nearing him even more.

Dexter stepped backwards and said, "Then why are you here?"

"I did my duty again, and they caught me this time. But it was worth it, 'cause, I had fed two birds with one seed, a twofer."

❝WHAT? ARE you out of your mind?" said Mark, jumping up from his couch as soon as Adam declared that he would visit his grandmother. The classic asymmetric wallpaper complimented the modern design of the den. For Adam, Mark's den was nothing new.

"I gave you the letter to let you know about her. You could have called her, sent her flowers, even. Don't go to that terrorists' country. They don't treat white people any good. I read this story about a guy that just vanished from that country. Poof. Gone. He didn't even get the chance to step out of the airport." Mark clapped his hands and continued, "Also, for your information, she doesn't even live in a city. You can't go by yourself. The place is practically an Atlantis. They don't even have any communication services: no Internet, no landlines. Cell phones don't even work properly there. Do they even know what cell phones are? The person I contacted to confirm about her letter being a word of truth had to travel to some nearby tiny village only to talk, so if you get lost, or worse, kidnapped, nobody would know about it."

"Are you finished or is there anything else you'd like to add?" While taking his usual place beside Mark's, Adam went on, "If you think I'm insane, then so be it, but you know very well that I've made my decision, and I'm not going back on it. So, wish me luck and help me prepare for it, will you?"

"Man, that's not being insane, that's suicide. You hear me? Suicide," Mark said, slapping his hand on the bar table.

"Suicide or not, I'm doing it. I came here to ask you to keep Wild while I'm gone. Can you do that for me?" inquired Adam.

"I've got mine to worry about, but they do get along fine. So yeah, I guess. But what if you never come back?" Mark leaned back.

"I will, at least I hope."

"And when exactly will you return?"

"Soon — I only wanted to ask a few questions, and as soon as I've got them answered, I'll return."

"That soon better be real soon, I can't keep your dog forever. When's your flight?"

"Not confirmed yet, I'm planning to leave by the end of this week," Adam answered.

"Put some tanning cream on your face and go sit by the sea, at least, try to blend in," Mark advised. "Did you call that guide mentioned in the letter?"

"Not yet. Will do it tonight."

He walked back to his car thinking about the things Mark had said. He knew that most of them were true. It was a dangerous adventure in all aspects, and he would venture a guess that nothing good would come of it, "What if my grandmother is one of them, the terrorists?" he said to himself. "I've decided — whatever happens, I'll manage. At least there'll be an adventure, some change in my life, and change is always good," he thought, convincing himself after five minutes.

19

FOR TWO long days Max had tried hard to be friends with Dexter. The loneliest person there and when he was this close. Rocky called him and said, "Hey you Max, come here."

Max walked across the hall and stood by the other side of his table; the table that had Rocky's name engraved on top. The table on which no one else would dare to sit.

"Yes."

"You think you're smart?"

"No."

"You are actually."

"Maybe."

"You want me to pick a fight?"

"No."

"You know the rules?"

"Whose rules?"

"Dammit."

"I mean the jailers or yours?"

"Still dammit."

"I wanted my counsellor to be happy, and I don't want any fight here."

Rocky reached out and grabbed his long curls twisting his other fist around his neck he said, "Then you must forget about what your counsellor said, and stick to my rules. Never talk to the newbie unless I approve. Got it?"

"Got it," Max whispered. Although his blood boiled and his veins felt the heat, he tried to look calmer; after a long time someone had grabbed his curls and he couldn't help but bring those nightmares back to life.

20

"MAY I speak with Mr Mujahid Khan, please?" said Adam, holding his mobile in between his ear and his shoulder.

"Assalamualaikum and yes, I'm speaking. Who is this?" Mujahid answered.

"I'm Adam Lyons."

"Oh, the grandson of Mamma. Hello Sir! How are you? I'm glad you called. What can I do for you Sir?" Said Mujahid, cutting his words in a delighted tone.

"I'm planning to visit my grandmother; she told me to call you. Can you guide me? What should I do? Where should I land? And can you pick me up, stuff like that?" Adam said, confused as for the different accent. He couldn't even recognise some words Mujahid used.

"Ah, that is so nice of you. I'm happy you

considered her request." Mujahid continued, "Sure, I can book you a ticket for Islamabad, our capital. Then I'll take you to her place with me, being your personal guide, it will take us about eighteen hours to reach it, but it's worth it, exquisite and scenic."

And with lots of terrorists too.

"By road? That wouldn't be great. Can't you book me to the place where Grandmother lives? I think that would be appropriate."

"There is a small airport at Gilgit. We can take another flight from Islamabad, but then, eventually you will have to take the road to reach Mamma, and one could only reach that place with a four-wheel drive."

"Oh, don't they have proper roads there? At least, a comfortable drive would be better if we are to travel by road," Adam said.

"Sorry Sir, there is no such road, only mud tracks."

"Can't she come and meet me in Islamabad?"

"She doesn't leave her place. She has promised to herself that she won't leave her ancestor's home for any reason. She is old and it's her wish. Besides, she told me she wants you to visit her yourself. That place is lovely and enchanting, and it's your right to know about your roots," said Mujahid.

Adam couldn't understand exactly what he was saying, but he told him to book the flight for next week, arrange the other things then let him know the details.

21

"WHOSE MISTAKE is this? Did you really think you could keep your wife out of this? She was a big part of this plan, and you can't just let her leave now," the man with a moustache said, sitting on a big office chair by a huge square table with lots of ornaments. The walls of the room had lots of paintings, probably expensive. Iman wondered if the guy was Ahmed's boss. His Asian features were the most prominent trait in his personality: dark black hair, black eyes, and brown skin with the most gruesome looks one could ever have. They had brought them inside with their faces covered so Iman didn't know which floor it was. As soon as they entered, the man started scolding at Ahmed.

"Don't you dare bring Iman in this; she doesn't know and I seriously don't want her to know," Ahmed said for the first time in the last twenty minutes, speaking with a harsh tone.

"Ah! Raising your voice in front of me?"

"Who the hell are you? You were just like me when you came here. They gave you all this, and they will take everything from you whenever they wish, like they did to the one before you; they always do this, and we are always stupid enough to fall into their trap, don't you see it now?"

"Yes! I know, and believe me, I have my own plans, and I am not as dumb as the last one. You'll see for yourself one day. Ah yes, I forget you have very little of your life left."

"What do you mean?"

"Man, since you haven't delivered the pack, I can't keep you; you're a threat to us. I seriously don't understand. As you stated before, that your wife brought the pack with her nine months ago, then why are you not delivering it?"

"I don't have it now! I told you the truth."

"Where is it? Lost in thin air?"

"That, I can't tell you!"

"Why so?" Ahmed looked away. The man continued, "I will not be lenient, so spill the beans."

No reply.

The man stood, came right up to Iman, grabbed her neck and said, "Did your husband introduce me? No! Let me do the honour; I am his beautiful boss Ahaan Ras, the king of New York. And did you know that your lovely husband used you to import a precious pack for us which he hasn't delivered yet, as promised."

"Stop!" Ahmed got up, but before he could reach Ahaan, the man standing right beside Ahmed grabbed him.

"I will kill you."

Iman struggled, his hand still wrapped around her neck. She tried to get out of his grasp, but his strong hand gripped her neck even tighter.

"This man over here is my childhood friend, but he leaves me no choice." He squeezed her wrist with his left hand and dragged her towards the door and into the lobby. Ahmed protested, yet couldn't do anything. The man holding him dragged him towards the other side of the lobby.

22

ADAM CLOSED his apartment's front door, still content to visit after a week since he first read the letter. He turned on the security locks, wheeled his small carry-on, pressed the button beside the elevator door and waited.

"Going somewhere?" inquired Anna from inside the elevator as soon as the door opened; Adam ignored her query and stepped inside.

"Still, not in a mood to chat? I only wanted to lessen your loneliness, nothing else."

"Who said I am lonely?"

"Are you not?"

"No, I have friends, and honestly I don't require your company to be happy," Adam replied without even looking at her.

"Ah, that I know. I only try. Is it wrong to even try?"

With the sound of the ping, the elevator's door opened again and Adam didn't waste a minute to get out.

23

"DO YOU *think I would send you to this private boarding school? Am I nuts? You can either rot inside your room or go to the public school the council has recommended. Choice is yours," his father snapped as soon as Max placed the brochure on his lap.*

"But, I would like to go," Max whispered, shivering and sweating. The salt water dripped over his eyes blocking his vision.

His father grabbed his small curls, twisted his head upwards and said, "Let me tell you what I would like to do. I would like to go to your principal and tell him you're not fit for schooling, and I would like to tell him you'd be better off in some psychiatric hospital that will treat you like a mad kid. That's what I would like to do. You want me to do that?"

"No."

"Then back off and don't make my life miserable anymore," said his father while letting him go with a jerk and

throwing the brochure, which went sliding down the narrow corridor and landed right at the mouth of his room.

Little Max slowly walked past the kitchen, which was barely two cabinets and a small room refrigerator, and through the narrow corridor. He picked the brochure up and banged the door of his room.

24

"I TRIED *Sarah, but he is not listening; he never does. I feel I will have to stay here forever, stuck with this man. I probably will never see you again. You are a dear friend; you have always listened to me. What will I do without you? Please don't go? Please for my sake, stay,"* Max said, wiping his tears with his small hands. They were sitting among their classmates as all the second grade students were to wait at the stadium until their teacher would announce who gets the chance to participate in that year's sports day. But both of them were least concerned about the happenings around. Sarah's parents had decided to send her to the boarding house not far away, but far enough for them not to be friends anymore.

"Don't cry. I will be back for my middle grades. Papa said he only wants me to go for a few years. I am sure you'll find some other friends. There will be new admissions in our grade next term," Sarah said.

"But, they always laugh at me and make fun of me. Nobody cares about being friends with me. Promise me you won't forget me. Promise me that we will be friends forever."

"Yes, we will, I Promise you that."

25

IMAN FELT drowsy, and her head throbbed. She did not remember how many days she had spent inside that small room; a single bed, with no windows and empty walls with only a toilet and a water tap in the corner. No one visited her. All she could hear were some footsteps rushing here and there. She never understood why, but they didn't even bother to open the door, nor did they give her any food. At first, she became so afraid that she tried to keep herself awake all night. She even tried to open the door, kicking it and making different sounds; hoping maybe someone would listen. Then, the lock twisted open, and Ahaan rushed in with a worried yet greedy look.

"Please..! Let me go, I did nothing." Words came out of her dry mouth as she placed her hands together.

"I will. You see, since I have locked you up our

enemies threatened us, they say they will attack us and destroy our reserves. We had been very busy increasing our security and sending them some nice messages from our side. The reason why I got no chance to appraise your beauty. Now I am here and I tell you..." Before Ahaan could finish his speech, a man entered the room. "They attacked us from the east side of the building."

Ahaan paced back, faster than he came in, leaving the door wide open. Iman stood up while gathering her courage; she had to find her husband. She had to find out if he was still in this building. She stepped out into the dark and empty lobby. Taking calculated steps, she walked towards her right, away from the east, wishing and praying.

One by one, she peeked inside the doors that came her way, and found them empty until the last one in the lobby; locked from outside. She twisted the round knob and found the person she badly wanted to see. By then, the deafening sound of the gunshots had filled the atmosphere.

"Alhamdullillah, you are safe," she said.

"Not for long. Are you okay? Did they do anything to you? Did they give you something to eat?" Ahmed said while hugging her.

"No, I am fine, what about you?"

"We must run while they are busy. I am sure they won't notice. If only I knew which wing they have attacked."

"East. They said someone attacked them from the east side."

"Let's go then. I know a secret gate towards west wing. The gate is inside a wall cabinet of the last room in the lobby downstairs, but first I need to find my bag and your ticket. Your flight's time is only a few hours away; if you hurry you could reach on time," Ahmed said.

"I am not leaving you."

"You have no choice." Ahmed took her hand and guided her out into the dark lobby. They walked past a few doors then Ahmed signalled her to stop. He slid open of the door, got inside and saw the last person they wanted to see.

26

"THESE PEOPLE are going to Pakistan?" Adam asked himself as he sat there waiting for his plane at the JFK Airport.

"Isn't it a country of illiterates and terrorists?" He had always imagined Pakistanis wearing large beards along with long white weird dresses like the ones he had seen on television, but that day, the picture was different. Some women were wearing long, black cloths over their head and body, but most of them were in pants and T-shirts. The men were freshly shaven. The Americans also seemed satisfied enough, willing to talk to the American sitting three seats away with a camera around his neck. Adam moved beside him.

"You travel to Pakistan a lot?" he said.

"Hello, and yes I do. I'm a photographer, and I adore beauty wherever it is."

"You find it safe enough? I heard a lot of terrorists live there."

"I won't deny it, but I haven't seen one yet, even though it's my fifth visit now."

"Have you visited any remote areas, like the northern Pakistan?" Adam asked. "They say most of them live there?"

"That's the only place I've been in Pakistan. The landscapes are beautiful," smiled the man.

Confused yet satisfied with an American's certification, Adam heard the boarding announcement, and everyone started walking towards the gate.

27

"EXCUSE ME, that's my seat. Can you please exchange yours with it?"

Adam heard those words, turned around and saw a woman standing all covered; she was talking to the person sitting in the middle with two elderly women. Apparently, her seat was beside Adam's, and she was asking the man to exchange it with hers.

What? How can a person like to sit beside those old women who'd annoy you to death and not sit with me? Leaving a window seat too? As if I'm a beast or something, Adam thought.

The man happily got up and sat on the seat by the window. Adam couldn't help staring at her. She had an elegance to her style. He noticed that she was not wearing those black robes; covered but with something more colourful than the rest, a light pink coat with a flower-patterned scarf.

"Assalamualaikum, do you have any problems? Please don't keep staring like that," she said looking straight into his eyes.

Adam turned, speechless. Those eyes — black, dark, mysterious and worried — as if they were telling strange stories.

Why was I staring at her? What's wrong with me?

28

"IMAN BLINKED as the tears draped down her soft cheeks merging into the printed flowers of her scarf. No matter how much she tried, she couldn't close her eyes. The pale face of her husband haunted her. Her worries did not end there; she had to answer to her family. What would she say to them? Why did she come back? What happened to her husband? Her head hammered as she sat in a plane, waiting for a new chapter to begin.

Then she noticed a man sitting to her left. Despite the crispness of the suit and the perfect tailoring, the man inside had dark blue eyes, filled with obvious pain and hidden trauma glistening in the tiny haze of light. At his lap was a case made of fine brown leather. His eyes were fixed on her, and she wondered why a man like him kept staring at her.

What should I do about it? Should I ignore him? Yes, I'll just ignore, she thought, but he stared and stared. She didn't know how she found the courage, for she looked straight into his eyes and said, "Assalamualaikum, do you have any problems? Please don't keep staring like that."

She closed her heavy eyes, and then she felt someone clutching her hands tightly. She opened her eyes again and found the elderly lady choking. She instantly stood up and held the lady's chest straight, patted her back with hard strikes. At last, the lady breathed again. Everyone stared at her. A little embarrassed, she sat on her seat again.

"Thank you, child," the lady said after a while.

"It was nothing," Iman said, nervously.

"What is your name, sweetie?"

"My name is Iman," she answered.

"Are you travelling alone?"

Iman opened her mouth but could not bring the words out. On a day like this, she had no answers at all. Least of all, she didn't want to bring back those terrifying memories of the day.

29

ADAM LISTENED to all that, but they were speaking some language he couldn't understand.

"I should have bought a language guide with me," Adam thought, closing his eyes. He heard her voice, sweet and soft.

"My child, I didn't leave you. I'm still with you. I'll always be by your side."

He opened his eyes and searched for the source, finding himself in a garden with lush green grass and trees with bright red apples. The mountains at the back, were majestic, surrounded by wispy clouds, and a waterfall. A woman sitting by the falls stretched her hands towards him. She had a white dress over her thin body. Her long black hair fell down her back. He walked closer until he saw his own reflection

— the same face cut, the lips and the nose. The only difference was her eyes. She had those big, black eyes… mysterious and dark.

"Mother?" he asked.

"Yes, my child. Come close. Sit with me."

Laying his head on her lap he said, "Where were you all this time? I needed you. I wanted to be with you. I don't know what it's like to be with you." He sobbed like a baby.

"I'm right here, by your side. I'm always here for you," she reassured and started reciting verses from the Qur'an. He could understand them, although it was in Arabic. Her voice comforted him, sweet and soft; something he hadn't heard before. He closed his eyes, listening to every word, majestic strong words, calling him to walk down the road towards heaven.

"Please put your seatbelts on. We're about to land." Adam woke up with those words.

Everything vanished — the beautiful scenery, the mountains, the clouds, and his mother. Putting his belt on, he sat up straight and waited for the plane to land.

Was it really a dream? Was she really my mother?

Adam longed for the answers to these questions. She was so beautiful. He felt her warm lap, her soft hands. It was enchanting. He closed his eyes to store those feelings in his heart, never to lose them, though it was just a dream.

"Maybe she wasn't my mother at all. How can she

be? I've never seen her alive, not in any photographs. She was reciting something in Arabic like the Muslims do — how would my mother know such things?" he whispered, yet it looked real; it felt real — all of it.

30

MAX CLOSED his eyes only to bring back the memories of that calm lake. The blue water and the plain land around the three sides of it always gave him the feeling he could never categorise it as a good or a bad one, just remorseful and happy at the same time. He never got away with the memories of that day. They just don't fade. They appeared in front of his eyes whenever his mind wished, glued with the memories of that lake.

"Son, go no farther. The lake is deep here, and the rocks are slippery; you will fall," his father said.

"Papa, its lovely, The fishes are dancing around the bread pieces. You should come here and see," Max said. He was happy that day when his father agreed to visit the lake. He had been more than happy, but his happiness didn't last long; it never did.

"Are you not listening? I will take you back home if you don't listen." His father grabbed him by his short curls and

dragged him away from the edge, but then at that moment his energy boosted and the emotions inside him boiled. He twisted his shoulders and stepped on his father's foot. His father screamed. Leaving the curls he started massaging his foot while balancing himself, but before his father could resume what he was doing, the hatred inside Max grew stronger, and he pushed him off the cliff into the deep and cold water.

DAM WALKED to the exit gate searching for a sign with his name. When he finally saw the person holding the sign, about twenty feet away, Adam Lyons didn't stop. He paced up and walked past him. The guy followed, asking if he was Adam Lyons.

Stop, you're not a coward, face it!

The guy's appearance was the reason why he was running. The moment he saw the man, that was it. Surely, the man had a suicide jacket right under the big shawl. He wore a short black beard and a white cap which Adam was sure he had seen one of the terrorists wearing in a TV report back home.

"Yes, I am Adam Lyons." He turned around to face the guy.

"Alhamdullillah,   at   last,   we   meet.

Assalamualaikum, I'm Mujahid Khan. Nice to meet you, Sir," he greeted.

"Oh yes, his name is Mujahid too. The terrorists here, they call themselves Mujahid," Adam whined softly, obscuring his fear with a smile. That man could be it. His brain worked faster.

Should he run inside and fly back right away? If he goes with this man, all of Mark's foresight could come true.

"Sir, are you alright? Is there a problem? I would love to help you. I'm here to help you," Mujahid said.

You — you're my problem.

Instead he said, "Have you arranged our seats for the domestic flight to Gilgit? Can you show me the ticket?"

Mujahid took two printed papers from his pocket and handed them to Adam.

He's wearing a jacket too. Can he pass the security here at the airport with all that?

Adam's head swirled from the dread he was experiencing. He had only seen this on the television screen before; it appeared more ghostly and dreadful when a man wearing all that, a carbon copy from television, stood in real life, right in front of him. He dared to look at the papers this Mujahid guy gave him. They were the ticket's, but should he trust the guy.

"Pardon my appearance Sir, I didn't get time

to change. It's Friday, a important day for Muslims. If you are having any second thoughts, then this is my ID card. Here, keep it, and I've also brought a recorded message from Mamma, your Grandmother," Mujahid said and handed Adam his phone.

This guy can read thoughts too.

Thoughts like these were making a permanent home in Adam's head, yet he played the message.

"Assalamualaikum, Dear Grandson. Welcome to a new world. I'm happy that you accepted my request. Mujahid is my dearest child, and you can trust him with your eyes closed, provided, that you trust me. He'll guide you to my place. You can ask him whatever you want to know. I'm sure he'll satisfy your inquiries. Waiting for you."

Her message ended with a beep. Adam handed back the phone.

His heart was beating hard. This time it was not fear or anxiety; it was something he couldn't explain, though he was sure it was blissful and pleasant. In an instant, he went with Mujahid. All his worries flew away, and he proceeded towards the domestic departure with a light heart.

"We have to hurry. Only fifteen minutes left for our boarding. Also I must warn you it's a small plane, so it will be a little bumpy," Mujahid warned.

"How do you speak English so well?" Adam asked.

"Well, I've done my doctorate from a reputable university here," Mujahid answered proudly.

"What... this guy is a doctor? I can't believe it," thought Adam. "Isn't it too early? You must be in your mid-twenties."

"No Sir, I look younger than I am. Twenty-eight years precisely."

"Oh, which subject?"

"Palaeontology."

"Fossils. Interesting."

"They are my life. I love to collect them, wherever I can find them. That's the reason why I wear these big jackets," he said and produced a handfull of fossils out of his pocket.

"Can you take these on the plane? They won't let you take those back in America."

"Well, I don't know. Let's try, I've never been on a plane before," Mujahid replied.

"Seriously?"

"Yes, and I would love to keep them. They are beautiful, aren't they?"

Adam didn't know what to answer, they were just rocks. To his relief they reached the customs counter before he could answer.

"Sir, you can't take these rocks with you," said the customs guy.

"These are no rocks, they are fossils. Isn't there any way I can?" Mujahid inquired.

"Then put them inside your luggage." The guy

pointed to Adam's suitcase.

Oh no, this can't be happening. What if they are bombs?

Mujahid looked at him blankly, "So, what do you say?" he said in a soft tone.

"Okay." Adam opened his suitcase to let him put the fossils inside.

They settled into their seats. To say that it was a small plane was an understatement. It was tiny, and smaller than any domestic plane he had seen in America. Everything inside was old and worn. Even the seat he sat on was crumbling.

"Are you sure this thing can fly?" asked Adam half convinced.

"They say so," Mujahid said pointing out to the airline logo.

"I've never been in this part of the world, never heard of it before this entire terrorism thing started. How do you live in such chaos? So many terrorists living here," Adam inquired after a moment.

"That's the biggest problem with our species; we propagate negative aspects of life more than the positive ones," Mujahid remarked.

"So, you are saying all that terrorism stuff is only drama?"

"No! Sir, not all of it; surely there's lots of exaggeration, that is. The percentage of the terrorism here is the same as in other parts of the world — we are not unique. Say, Sir, don't you have places in your country where one cannot go without protection?" Adam nodded. Mujahid smiled and continued, "Just like that, we have some areas that are not safe. The rest of our country is safe for everyone."

"What about the place we are going?"

"Safe enough Sir — safer than any other place. The people are very generous and kind-hearted."

"Please don't call me Sir. I have a name, and I would like you to call me Adam."

"Okay then, Adam it is. You are an architect right? How do you find our country's architecture up till now?"

"Very different from what I had perceived."

"I don't know about anything else, but I'm confident that you will like the place we are going. Its architecture is something different, amazing stonework. Mamma's prized possession. She inherited her fortress. It's over one hundred years old."

"Seriously, no one told me that before."

Finally, something more interesting than meeting with the old lady.

"Why do you call my Grandmother, Mamma? What's her name?" Adam asked after a while.

"Her name is Badr-un-Nissa. In case if you are wondering if I am her son, I'm not, I'm only a guy she took care of. She kind of adopted me when she came back home. It's a long story I'll tell you some other day," said Mujahid.

"Wait, her name was what? Is she a Muslim? Was my mother a Muslim too?" Adam almost shouted.

"Well, yes, she is a Muslim, I don't know about your mother. Maybe you should ask Mamma."

Adam sat there, processing what he had just heard. If his mother was a Muslim, how come his father married her? Why didn't he know? It's a big secret to keep. How did he miss it? The news was frustrating him down to his spine. He was repeatedly redefining the gained knowledge in his mind. His Grandmother was a Muslim; all of this could be a trap. What if she would force him to accept Islam? What if that was her basic plan? Muslims can hypnotise people. He was travelling to a Muslim country without even thinking of the possibility that his Grandmother could be a Muslim too. He felt as if he was falling, only to be ambushed by the Beast.

32

"ADAM, SIR, we have to move out. The plane has landed." Adam came back to the present. He moved towards the exit, still thinking. What should he do about it?

"Oh, this place — it's wonderful," Adam whispered as he stepped out of the plane. He could feel the cool breeze, and see huge mountains at the back. His eyes ran along the entire runway at the edge of the slope. He turned towards Mujahid, who was walking alongside him.

"The runway is too small, isn't it?"

"Yes, it is. Gilgit, Baltistan is all hills and mountains. This is what they can manage here. They use only small planes like ATR or Fokker; the larger planes don't operate from here. Major flights come from Islamabad only," Mujahid answered with a smile.

"These mountains, they are huge, aren't they?"

"Well, Gilgit, they call Baltistan the home of five eight-thousander mountains, with many smaller ranges. We have three of the longest glaciers in the world. Outside the polar region, that is," said Mujahid.

"That's new."

"There is a lot of new stuff here. Just keep your heart open, and you'll get what you desire." Mujahid pointed towards the seats and said, "Sir, please take a seat here, and I'm going to look for our ride."

"Okay, but please call me Adam."

"Oh, Yes. Adam," Mujahid headed towards the exit.

Adam glanced at the surroundings. A simple yet clean environment. He could see very few travellers, almost none foreign.

"Sir, do you want a ride?" asked a man in jeans.

"Oh, my ride is being arranged already," he said.

"Okay, is this your first time here?"

Adam hesitated, "Yes..."

"Welcome Sir, my name is Khalid Jan. I work here as a taxi driver. What's your name?" said Khalid.

"A taxi driver? That's nice, I'm Adam," he deliberately excluded his last name.

"You must be wondering how come a taxi driver speaks English, right?" Adam nodded, "Well, sir, thanks to the government here, they educated everyone. We are more educated and modern than before, and our literacy rate has exceeded over seventy percent. Gilgit is one of the most educated regions in northern Pakistan."

"Oh, that's..."

"Let's go. Our ride is waiting outside," Mujahid came back. He noticed Khalid and said, "Oh! Assalamualaikum, brother."

"Wàlikumassallam," Khalid replied before leaving.

"You didn't even ask who he was. Do you know him?" Adam asked after they walked away.

"Nope, not really, but I can guess he's one of the taxi drivers, right?" indicated Mujahid.

"Yes," Adam said.

The ride waiting outside was a Jeep. A nineteen fifty's ford had a leather hood, outdated, yet well maintained. They settled in the front.

"When exactly will we reach the place?" Adam asked, staring out the window.

"Well, we can't say precisely. Most of the roads are barely paved, and the area is full of landslides. I hope we don't get one on our way. Then we could reach our destination in about six hours."

"Sir, I think you should stay for the night at Raikot Bridge. There is a place called Hotel Shangrilá. It will be sunset by the time we reach there, and you know how the roads are. We can't travel at night," protested the driver.

"Oh, no, I can't waste one day only because it's night," Adam raised his voice.

"But he's right, Adam. We can't travel in those areas at night. We have to stay. Besides, take some rest before all the bumping and the jolting starts," said Mujahid.

"Why didn't you tell me before?"

"Well — my fault. You know that was my first flight, so I never considered that it would take us this much time to travel by airplane. As they say, it's only an hour flight, but they never mention that the check-in and check-out would take so much time."

"Oh, okay then," said Adam, turning towards the roads and the scenery. He noticed that everything turned brown and rocky, not to mention the temperature was rising. The water of the river by the road became brown and muddy. To his surprise, the road was good.

"You said the roads are not good here. This road is perfect."

"This is the highway that connects us with the rest of Pakistan and China. We are nearing Chillas; it's in between Naran and Gilgit. The roads I was talking about will start after Raikot Bridge. That is the Fairy Meadow's zero point. We'll start our real journey from there tomorrow. Mamma lives in a small valley. It's beautiful, but far away, deep into the mountains. Hey, did I mention before that Chillas is full of Buddhist sculptural art?" said Mujahid.

"Oh, that's nice. What about the weather? The heat is increasing. Is it really hot there?" asked Adam.

"No, the weather is lovely there, but the journey towards it is a trip to hell."

Adam's shoulder cramped and his backbone hurt when they reached the hotel after an hour. Their Jeep pulled over at the mouth of a three-way junction splitting up equally where the man-made constructions were little; only some shops across the road and a hotel to their left were visible. A typical northern construction with a red pagoda, and plain, white walls, complemented with a nice lawn and trees of fruits like apple and apricot.

"Please take a seat here. It's Maghrib time, our sunset prayer. I'll be back soon," Mujahid said, pointing towards the metal lawn chairs.

"Is it safe?" Adam was sure if he sat out there, he'd encounter thieves or worse — terrorists.

"You'll be fine. These people are friendly enough and most of all, they are used to having foreigners around," Mujahid reassured and went straight towards a place Adam didn't recognise. The building was square just like any church; the only difference was the weird pillars that stood on all four sides. It looked divine. People were going towards it in groups. There came a sound — exquisite, sweet and enchanting. The more he listened to it, the more he became bewitched. It was like magic, compelling. He got up and walked towards the building. People were washing themselves at a place besides the building. There were a lot of taps on a huge thick pipe. Mujahid was sitting on a stool made of concrete, busy in the exact process everyone else was using to wash. Everything was orderly and organised. Then they peacefully walked inside the building, so he neared the place and peeked from a window.

How could they do that?

They were simply standing in an orderly manner, shoulder to shoulder, as if they were waiting for something to start. Then he heard the sound; first a loud one, then it became soft and low.

This sound. I've heard it before. This is interesting. I'll ask Mujahid what this is all about. Oh, what am I doing here?

Adam turned around to go back to his seat. Then, he heard the loud sound again, and every single person inside the building bowed down simultaneously in a position that symbolised surrender.

"Oh, it's beautiful. I should stay and watch all these steps, surely that can't be bad. They all look so much in peace," Adam thought. He was so lost by the sight that he forgot to run to his place, even after the prayer ended and everyone moved out.

"You should have come inside. It's more enchanting," Mujahid said, his eyes twinkling in awe.

"Oh, I was fine here," he said as if he'd been caught stealing.

33

NEXT MORNING, Adam's face was shining yet his urge for truth grew stronger and stronger. The conversation the night before caused a wide grin to break across his face.

"So, I was wondering what that was all about. Not any act of terrorism. Or was it a camouflage?" Adam had been waiting long to ask these questions, but he didn't have time until dinner the night before.

"Well, sir, not at all camouflage or anything near. It's our way to thank Allah. This is our humble way to pray to God. We do it five times a day to remember his superior being and to thank Him."

"Five times a day—that's an awful lot with the long procedure, provided that one has to go out to pray. By the way, I saw no women. Don't they pray?"

"Sure, they do. They are not obliged to pray in a mosque;

they do it in their homes."

"Oh, so at least one thing that heard before is correct. Muslims keep their women at home, right?"

Mujahid smiled, "Let me explain with an example. If you have a precious stone that's beautiful yet delicate, what would you do? Would you take it wherever you go, or would you try to protect it and keep it hidden in a safe or something?"

"I would be a fool if I didn't protect it with my life."

"Women are that precious stone, in Islam. We cherish them with our heart and protect them from the evil world, yet it doesn't mean they don't get out and have a social life; they do. Covered and protected, they do lots of things. Sometimes more than men," explained Mujahid.

"What about all that washing stuff? It looked like you all did the same process. Is it mandatory?"

"The Wadu. Yes. It's like going on a date with God. Wouldn't one get prepared before that? We wash and clean ourselves."

"Hmm, What about the dressing? All of you were wearing stuff the suicide bombers wear on television. Don't get offended, but my image about you guys was far towards terrorism than any humble beings. It seems like I was wrong."

"Why would I get offended? About the terrorist thing, I don't think you're any different from anyone else; just watching television back home, seeing what they want you to see. You can't say how anything tastes only by looking at it. Take a step and try it for yourself. The dress, Shalwar Khameez, is an Asian dress. Muslims in Saudi Arabia dress differently. So in other parts of the world."

"Ah, you know it seems funny now, but the moment I had set eyes on you back at the Airport, wearing all that, with a huge jacket, I was damn sure you're one of the terrorists," Adam said with a weak smile.

"You're not the first one even in my country. Although people know how Islam works, they still blame the Muslims for extremism. The terrorists around the world are not Muslims, Christians, or Jewish; they are Extremist. None of these religions promote violence. If you compare these religions' bad deed list, it would be the same. How can a follower of Almighty Allah be so heartless? Plus, every religion forbids suicide."

"Maybe you're right. One more thing, what was he reciting? The loud one in the beginning, I think I've heard it before."

"It's called Azan. Allah has taught us a way to call all the Muslims towards him, to tell them it's prayer time. Maybe you've heard it on television," Mujahid answered.

"Adam, our ride is here, let's go."

Adam came out of his thoughts and found Mujahid standing by his side, "Okay."

They hopped into the Jeep. All three of them squeezed in the front. Adam purposely sat by the window.

"Sir, the ride is a little bumpy; please be careful," said the driver.

"Aren't these lots of water bottles? It's five or six hours' drive, right?" Adam inquired

"Yes, it is but mostly hot and dry. Plus, there isn't any shops on our way. Everything is hot, even the streams coming from the rocks."

"Really?" Adam said, wondering how hot can it be. It's just a few hours' ride, and this place's temperature was fine enough for him. The Jeep moved steadily on the road. There wasn't anything or anyone except their Jeep, just brown sandy rocks and the mountains. No sign of life.

"Isn't it amazing. The water is flowing with all these stones and rocks, yet, it's all muddy and brown," Adam wondered out loud.

"It's the river Indus – it's brown all the way to the Arabian Sea. No matter what the surroundings are, it sure is amazing stuff."

"Hmm, oh, are we going to travel over that bridge?"

"Yes, we are."

"No way that's suicide, look at it, it's falling apart. Tell me it's not functional, right?" exclaimed Adam.

"Sir, it's been like this for years now, it sure is functional. I use it daily," answered the driver.

"But, I'm not travelling on it. I'm not stupid enough to do so. See, the panels are shaking badly," said Adam

"Sir, this bridge is old, but it's safe. I assure you, we'll be fine," Mujahid said.

"If you like, you can walk through it, and I'll bring the Jeep afterwards."

"Well, it's a long bridge to walk all the way

through; I think if you're insisting, I'll be fine."

Adam was not at all convinced, but he said otherwise. The bridge looked very weary and old, a hanging bridge. He had seen many on their way from Gilgit; every time they drove past one, he would wonder how anyone would travel on these.

When the Jeep finally started its way through the bridge, there came an odd or rather dramatic screeching sound of iron along with the patterning of the wood panels. For the first time, Adam experienced the sense of fear. Fear of losing his life. He wanted to cross, as it was the only way he would be with his grandmother, yet his heart pounded.

"Oh my, some panels are missing. How can you drive over them?"

"Yes sir, but we'll be fine," the driver said with half-smile.

"Are you sure?"

"Just close your eyes," Mujahid suggested.

He closed his eyes and the world started to revolve around him. The wind blew through the Jeep, adding another sound to the atmosphere; whistling through his ears, rectifying the fact, loud and clear, that he had been driving through his death rope.

"You can open your eyes now, we're off the bridge," Mujahid said, looking at Adam's clenched hand.

"That's it? We are back on the road?" Adam opened his eyes and saw a small track by the edge, smaller than a single track road and their Jeep was covering it all.

Thankfully, Adam sat on the side where he couldn't see much of the road's edge or the depth of the valley. Still, the jarring was making him feel as if he would bounce off the Jeep soon.

"The road, it's much too narrow, isn't it?" Adam said.

"It sure is — small track, but safe. I drive through these areas almost daily, so I'm used to its trials. I remember them by heart, don't worry," explained the driver.

"It's easy for you to say. From where I stand, I fear that we actually can travel through this track. So how much time will it take us to cross it? I'm sure it's just a patch, right? Rest of the road is better?"

"Well, Adam, the road is even worse than this one. I'm sure we'll cover it. This is the only reason I didn't have an exact time frame for our trip."

"Seriously? There's something worse than this? Besides, you should have warned me beforehand."

"I did, I told you, the roads are not good. Didn't I?"

"Not good. This is the worst."

"Yes, but see the brighter side; you will meet your grandmother. Isn't it something?"

"I always wondered why she couldn't travel to meet me... now I know."

The track was winding up the hill. To his surprise, he saw another bridge, smaller. It was a hanging bridge with panels of wood and thick ropes. The Jeep stopped at the mouth.

"Don't you dare tell me we will go through this one too? This is worse than the last one," Adam burst out.

"Sir, it is a little dangerous for us to ride in the Jeep. You must get out and pass it by foot, and I'll bring the Jeep afterwards," informed the driver.

"Don't worry, I'll be on your side," ensured Mujahid.

"I'm not an adventurous person yet I'm enjoying the thrill, so why not? Let's walk through it," Adam said, while calming himself down. "They do it every day. How hard can it be?"

Getting out of the Jeep was easy; taking his first step on that rickety bridge was hard. To Adam, a mile's walk on the bridge looked long enough. Most of the panels were missing, and the iron had rust on it.

"I can do this." With a firm belief and determination, he stepped ahead. Suddenly, his worries vanished; a refreshing breeze hit him and he felt peaceful.

Once they crossed the bridge, Adam sat at the edge of the cliff and waited for the Jeep; he glared at it as it rocked the bridge. He was lost in the mesmerising sight, enough to forget about the fact that down to his front, right under his feet, stood the sheer drop to the valley with brown and muddy river flowing. The bridge shook badly even after the Jeep drove past Adam.

"Do you want to see the Buddhist sculptural art? It's a little detour from here, but not very far. Should we stop by?" Mujahid asked, as soon as they were back on track.

"Well, okay if it's nearby."

"Let's go," Mujahid said to the driver.

After five minutes of driving, they came across the huge stone. The exposed flat surface of it stood right in front of him; the enormous structure of the stone stood in the middle of nowhere. The carving showed triangular human hunters hunting for the animals a lot bigger than them.

"You know most of these rocks dated even before 1000 BC," said Mujahid.

"Really, that old? This is interesting."

Adam's philosophical mind ruminated about things like why man had always wandered about for food. A necessity, yet not needed. Why did humans forget that the most important hunger is of their souls.

34

"ADAM, LET'S go. It's a long journey ahead and a tiring one too," Mujahid tried to pull him out of his thoughts, but it took him awhile to process his words.

"What are you saying exactly? A long journey? Argghhh, you are giving me goosebumps."

"Well, it's a four-hour drive, but the route is sometimes uncertain. Don't worry; it won't take us over four hours, but we have to keep the margin for any inconvenience."

"Okay, let's go then."

They hopped into the Jeep and started their journey again. The temperature was rising constantly. The scenery became drier and more yellow; rocks and hot sand everywhere.

"I can see the reason for needing all those bottles of water for just a few hours' drive — it's like hell,"

Adam said.

"Well, it sure is hot here." Mujahid produced a slight smile on his face.

"Tell me, it's not getting hotter than this," Adam said, wishing the answer to be in his favour.

"Not much sir," said the driver.

"Oh, I don't think I can bear any more heat now," sighed Adam. The Jeep was bumping around through the stony path, shaking everyone. There was nothing, not even a single plant.

"We have left the river's side?" Adam asked.

"Yes, we'll catch it back again after we go down the mountain but not this big one. We'll be going towards one of its branches, in fact, we are heading towards its mouth," Mujahid answered.

"What do you mean? Does my grandmother lives on a mountaintop?"

"Yes, it's not exactly up on the top. A twenty minute hike to get there."

"Oh my, you didn't mention this before either," Adam said, devastated.

How can this guy manage without revealing so much information?

"I didn't mention it before only because I desperately wanted you to meet Mamma. She's my fairy godmother, my Mother Teresa; I want her to be happy. The moment she told me about her wish to meet you, I became desperate to bring you here."

"And you thought if you told me the details I would have run away?" Adam said.

"It's just a little hike. The path is intact. You'll enjoy it. It's over a thousand years old. They carve the cliff into stairs; most of the path is still intact."

"That old?"

"I told you it's a historical place, and you'll love it"

The Jeep jolted down the mountain; it was a harsh ride down, but then Adam heard the sound of screeching brakes, and their Jeep almost hit something coming from up the hill. He looked up and saw a large amount of small rocks sliding down. The driver abruptly reversed the Jeep, until it was clear from the sliding area.

"What was that?" Adam inquired.

"Landslide. Just pray that this doesn't block the road," replied the driver.

Adam quietly waited, looking through the Jeep's windscreen; the rocks fell down, taking heaps of sand with them. Mystical and fearsome. They waited for about five long minutes. Slowly dust settled, and the damage by the landslide became visible.

"Do you think we can cross the road now?" Mujahid inquired.

"No, wait a little more."

"How little? Should we go back?" Adam said.

"I'm going on foot to check it out," said the

driver and hopped out.

He came back after a minute and started the engines. "It's fine, let's go now."

The Jeep jolted on the ragged road over numerous painful bumps. They took a sharp turn downwards and entered a very narrow area covered with high rising cliffs.

As the Jeep moved deep into the valley, Adam saw an uninterrupted waterfall coming from the top of the cliff on his left; the fall was almost two hundred feet high. He couldn't even see its mouth. The burbling sound of the water falling on the bare rocks created an enchanting scene, and the temperature suddenly lowered. The only missing element was any sign of life. Wherever there is water, there is always life, but here the water fell on hard rocks making a little pond that turned into a stream, going straight towards the river Indus, without a single patch of greenery.

The driver stopped the Jeep near the pond.

"We have to walk past the stream. Our man is waiting at the bottom of the stairs with a pony to carry your luggage," Mujahid informed.

"Okay," said Adam. "This place is so enchanting. It feels like someone has switched off the heater and switched on the air conditioner."

"Yes, no doubt about it. Did you notice that on our way here, there were lots of streams and falls, yet they were not at all making any difference? But here, it's different," said Mujahid as he took Adam's carry-on from the back of the Jeep.

"Seriously, I'm astonished. I don't know about your God, but surely there's somebody who's responsible for all this," added Adam.

"Sir, it's time for me to say goodbye now. It's been a pleasure travelling with you." The driver raised his hand for farewell.

"Pleasure's all mine. I enjoyed every bit of the trip."

They shook hands, and with that the driver left them standing by the stream. They crossed the water and walked. Right beside the fall was a structure of stairs carved into the cliff. Although the angle of the cliff was almost eighty degrees, the zigzag stairs looked good for hiking.

"Assalamualaikum. Welcome, sir," said a man standing by the stairs.

"Wàlikumassallam. This is Khadim; he's Mamma's butler."

"Oh, hello! Nice to meet you," Adam said. Khadim started fixing his luggage to the pony with the help of a cotton rope.

"Let's climb up," Mujahid said.

"This is very interesting; these stairs are finely carved," admired Adam.

"We don't know specifically which era but it's surely older than a thousand years. The Chinese T'ang dynasty first built the fort when they made an alliance with Gilgit Baltistan's ruler back in the eighth century. They made these stairs long after that."

"What fort?"

"Oh, didn't I mention before? Mamma lives in a fort of her ancestors."

"No, you didn't tell me. Really?"

"Yes, its history is complicated. I'll tell you someday."

"Sure, I would love to know about the historic place my mother belonged to," Adam said, astonished by the piece of information he had just heard.

8th century means it must be a Buddhist architectural design, and my grandmother owns it. That's surely interesting.

Lost in his thoughts he forgot about the fact he had been climbing up the cliff and was almost at the top.

35

ADAM HAD never been this close to any elderly lady before; the feeling of being with family subdued with the immense current between them. She sat in front of him, on a sofa, a book on her lap, her clothes like nothing he'd ever seen; some kind of a smock, with neatly embroidered panels at front — colourful. Her wrinkled hands were still beautiful, strong and confident.

The instant his eyes met hers, he noticed the same black eyes — dark and mysterious, the ones he'd seen in his dreams. She smiled, a very meaningful smile, as if his presence had made her speechless, obscuring her overwhelming emotions. They both sat in front of each other for ten long minutes, never uttering a single word, looking at each other, finding their own spirits between one another.

There weren't any windows, only one door, the one he had entered from, yet the room was brightly lit. He glanced up to see the source of light. It was a square opening in the middle of the roof. Not just an opening, but with mirrors by its sides, reflecting the bright sunlight inside the room. A brilliant way to avoid the chilling wind and get the sun's bright light in. Smiling at the roof, he moved his eyes back to hers. Finally the silence broke; she said the enchanting words — words that could melt almost anything.

"Come dear Grandson. Hug your ever-waiting Grandmother; it's been a long wait for me. Come, together we'll make all things right."

36

ADAM RECALLED the anxiety that enriched in every grain of his body the moment he stood there, right at the last step, for a long minute, trying to let out of the sudden shock. He couldn't even find the courage to ask himself.

I've seen this place before.

Then he remembered the dream — the first ever dream that felt real; the same white hut with a red curved roof, the same carved door and the knob, a big round flower at the middle of the door. The only difference was the lovely surroundings; to his left, the enchanting waterfall and to his right, a small field of vegetation. Right in front of him, in the centre of the platform, was the fort, behind the white hut, a stone structure with wood carvings. The water flowing down the cliff felt enormously huge. Adam searched for its crest, but the clouds broke his vision. It was a natural platform almost at the middle of the cliff. The temperature decreased ten times as soon as he stepped on the platform.

37

"THE SUPPER is served," informed Khadim after an hour of their arrival. Adam and his grandmother, still sitting in the library, surrounded by lots of books, silently observed one another.

"Let's go to the dining hall, Baita." Mamma got up and walked past Adam, still blown away by her presence. He couldn't believe the mere sight of her; it was real, she was real, and she was his grandmother.

How come she's my Grandmother? She's totally a native Pakistani, he thought.

Yet, there was something compelling between them; he could feel it.

"Son, are you not hungry?" Mamma inquired.

"Yes," Adam replied, although his hunger was far different from the one she was referring. Then again without asking any of the questions, he got up and followed her.

They crossed the new construction and entered the old fort connected by a narrow lobby and a set of stone stairs. It was a huge square with no windows and an opening at the middle of the roof. Same structure as the library, only its construction was older, and it had another door on the far side of the room connecting it with the kitchen. The walls were made of stones with a pattern of wooden panels in between. In the middle of the room, two steps below, was a large but low table at the centre of the room, and one had to sit on the floor to eat. The kind Adam had seen in Chinese movies.

"Please, here," Khadim pointed towards a place near Mamma.

"It's a very nice place. I would love to know about its history — interesting stuff," Adam said while taking his place.

"Sure, it is. Mujahid will tell you all about it tomorrow morning InshaAllah," ensured Mamma.

"Assalamualaikum, I'm sorry for being late," Mujahid apologised and sat opposite Adam.

"This is amazing. The food, it's like pizza. What it's called?" Adam inquired as soon as he took his first bite.

"It's called Chap Shoro. It's a local dish, and it's Khadim's specialty," answered Mujahid.

"So, what exactly do you know about your mother?" Mamma started the topic Adam was desperate to bring about.

"Only that she was a Pakistani, and she died when I was born." Adam sighed, opened his mouth and shut it again.

"If you are wondering about something, then you should ask; I'm here to answer your questions," said Mamma.

"Well, it's just your accent. Is it British? You seem like a native Pakistani; how did you learn to speak like this?" said Adam.

"I've lived in Scotland most of my married life. Are you aware of the fact that your mother had never been to Pakistan? She was born in Stirling and lived there all her life. She became a doctor from the Stirling University. She met your father there. What a pleasant time it was," said Mamma.

"Wait a second... my father has been to Scotland? That's not possible. He never mentioned it," said Adam, with astonishment.

"Did you even know your father was a doctor too?"

"That can't be true. No, maybe I'm not your grandson at all; how am I not aware of this basic information about my father? If he was a doctor, then why was he running a construction business? This is insane." Adam left the room. Mujahid followed him and said, "Adam, please, listen to her. She's got proof, you are her Grandson. Let me show you... your father's photographs... they are here in the library."

"Okay." Adam calmed himself down and went

inside.

"Look. There's your father with your mother on their graduation day." Mujahid took the framed photograph off the wall and showed it to him,."That's your father, isn't it?" Mujahid asked.

"Yes, he sure is my father," Adam murmured.

"Your father didn't tell you anything about his life, maybe because it devastated him, and maybe he was desperate to keep you away from the life he'd been living. I don't know the reason, but I always wondered why," clarified Mamma while taking her seat on the couch.

"Sorry I acted so absurd," whispered Adam.

"No, my dear grandson, it's entirely my fault; I should have at least waited until morning. You are tired now," sighed Mamma.

"I'm not at all tired. Maybe I am tired of lies and misguidance, but I need to know the truth," Adam said, while putting his hands over his face.

"Well, I don't have answers why your father never told you anything or what was his story, but I have my daughter's diary. I'm sure it will at least satisfy you till her death," she said with prominent signs of agony on her face.

"Here, you can read it," she added, after placing the big red book titled with his mother's name on his lap.

38

DEAR DIARY,

My name is Sarah Lyons. This is a story of how I became Sarah Lyons from Sarah Amir, in barely two months. It's been a year and a half now. I'm writing this story to fulfil my loving husband's humble request. He's gifted me this beautiful diary to write in, as I have nothing to do for a while. After being so busy with my clinics, I'm now on bed rest for the rest of my pregnancy, waiting for my unborn to arrive into this lovely world.

Well, where should I start? I'd seen David Lyons several times during my university. He was my senior. We were poles apart; always crossing each other's way in the university campus, but never uttering a word. I was a Muslim; he was Christian. I kept my distance from men; he was always with women. He was bold; I was shy. For him, I never existed; out of his league. A girl wearing hijab has nothing to do with a man like him. Yet,

I knew a few things about him like his name and that he was a popular yet hard-working student.

It all started in the last semester at university. My teacher assigned me to do an internship in the outskirts of a small town, near the University, with one of my seniors and that particular senior happened to be him.

At first father did not approve, but then he softened knowing that my entire past year's hard work and battle to get through it would be flushed away. My teachers insisted in that, and I had no choice but to comply. It was a forty-days camp. We had to assist the community hospital doctor in a town away from home. Father booked a room in a guest house near the hospital. I had a feeling beforehand something different would happen, and it would change my life once and for all.

"Hello sweetie, how's life?" David raised a sneer on his face as soon as I entered the camp room. It was a small room right beside the doc's office. When I didn't reply or even look at him, he burst out loud, "Am I invisible? Or worse, are you deaf?" turning all red.

"Hi. Of course I heard you," I whispered.

"Oh, so you aren't deaf yet."

"Yet?"

"Tell me you know me."

"Of course, you're my senior and your name is David Lyons."

"How interesting. Nothing other than that?"

"There isn't anything other than that."

"Yeah, yeah sure," his grin grew bigger than before.

At last the Doctor called us. We went in and started our day's work.

Working with him around was annoying as hell. I had to keep reminding myself of our norms and values. He was like a magnet that attracts every woman on his path. Talking with the female patients in his American accent, or rather impressing them with his charm, was a part of his everyday job description.

I always hated these kinds of men. My views about the guy changed instantly. If I had a tiny bit of attraction towards him, all of it vanished. The most annoying part of all this was his attitude towards me; he was devastated by my actions. He had never seen a girl who doesn't care about him. This made him more desperate to break down my walls, and have a nice little time with me.

"Why don't you talk? Am I not good enough for you?" He kept asking questions like this.

One day, I was working with the doctor, discussing some patients. He came in and sat beside me. I was so flustered that I sprang up from the sofa, and my heart sped.

"Is there a problem, Sarah?" the doc asked.

"No Sir, I just wanted a glass of water," I lied. When I came back with a glass of water, I deliberately sat on a single chair beside the doc.

"What exactly is your problem?" David grabbed my wrist and twisted it hard as soon as we were out of the building.

"Leave me alone," I gasped and tried to get out of his grip.

"I will not leave you until you give an explanation here."

"What kind of explanation do you want?"

"Why do you ignore me?"

"Haven't you noticed I ignore every man?"

"No. Not everyone. You seem to have a soft spot for the doc." He clenched his teeth.

"He's not just anyone; he's my boss these days, plus he's my father's age. There's a big fat difference."

"Okay, so you'll talk if I'm practically deformed, right?"

"No. Not even then, I won't." With that I stormed out, but he rushed after me, stomping his feet, observing my every move with rage and fury.

Adrenaline rushed through my veins; I quickened my pace and tried to get away from him. Fear gripped me as I realised that I was alone with him on the dimly lit street.

"For God's sake, tell me how can I get to know you better. It's eating me alive," he begged as he grabbed my elbow, dragged me to a stop, and made me face him. He shook my shoulders and his face twisted in a pleading expression.

I stammered over my words, and blurted out, "I won't talk unnecessarily to any man who isn't a brother or uncle or my father or husband. You aren't a Mehram. It's the basic teachings of Islam."

I lifted my confusion while he let me go, his lips stretched into a smile as he turned around and left.

I stared at his retreating figure as he made his way back towards the building. My heartbeat slowly returned to normal as my breathing steadied.

After that day, he never bothered me again. I was happy with his transformation. He became soft; never speaking unless required and sitting quietly most of the days. Then, within a week, I got agitated. His tranquillity killed me more than his anger. I was at ease with his fury more than his composure. Thankfully, I obscured my feelings, and the nightmare ended at last. My life returned to normal. Too normal.

Until one day, I opened the front door of my house and found him right in front of me. I lost all of my breath. Then, gracing my ears and reaching down to my soul were the most enchanting words he could ever uttered. That phrase echoed in my head as I tried to make sense of what he had just said…

"Assalamualaikum!"

I felt numb.

"May I speak to your father?"

"Who's at the door, Sarah?" I heard my father from behind.

I ran straight up to my room and locked myself in. I don't know how much time I spent under my pillow.

"Sarah, open the door," my mother ordered, while knocking at the door. It felt like thunder. I don't know how I found the courage to open the door for her.

"Do you love him?" Her words pierced right into my heart.

"No, mother, it's not like that. I don't even know him," I blurted out, almost in a whisper. Tears came to my eyes. I knew Father would be mad at me. He would think I'd broken his trust, that I'd had kept relations with a man.

"Don't worry, my child. David told us everything. Your father and I are not mad at you. We just wanted to know. Do you love him? He has asked for your hand Downstairs,

and convinced your father he'll take good care of you." Mother produced a cheerful grin.

"What are you talking about? That's impossible. He's not Muslim," I said, confused as hell.

"No, my dear he was not Muslim then, but he is now. He has asked your father's permission to meet you," Mother replied.

"Is father even considering his proposal?" I was dumbstruck as I heard the impossible words from my mother's mouth.

"Yes, he is." Mother smiled.

"Seriously?" I muttered slowly.

"He had sent me to ask you if you want to meet him."

"Should I?" I inquired with disbelief.

"It's your decision darling. We'll be okay with any decision you make."

"Today?"

"Yes. David's insisting. I think he is desperate."

"Okay, I'll be down in a minute."

"Please, wash your face and change into something nice. But, don't forget to wear a hijab."

"Of course!"

Mother left me with a mixture of emotions. Half scared and half happy - nervous as hell. When I descended the stairs, Mother was waiting for me at the bottom, blissfully smiling. I felt butterflies in my stomach. I saw him standing by the sofa with a certain humbleness in his posture. He looked different.

"Assalamualaikum," he said again with a beautiful smile on his face. His face was shimmering with hope. His eyes had *something special in them, pure and simple.*

"So, don't you have questions?" at last he broke the silence.

"Why?"

He smiled, and kept on staring the floor. Then I realised that this was the difference between the David I met a month ago and the one who was sitting right in front of me.

"You — you inspired me. The fact that you let no one come in between you and your values inspired me. When I left you that night, I dug into Islam. From the beginning I never found it wrong in any sense. It's a complete Deen. I'm so glad I came across you."

"No. Please correct yourself here. It's you. Your efforts changed you for the greater good. I only gave you the hint, as I always do to others. They don't seem to take it the way you did."

"You honestly remember nothing, do you?" he asked.

"Remember what?" I said, dumbstruck.

"The day when I first asked you Why you kept your distance from men, almost fifteen years ago."

"Fifteen years? No, no, you're mistaking me with someone else, beside, you came here from America for your medical degree, didn't you? You're an American."

"I sure am, but my family moved here for a year when I was in middle school."

"Don't tell me you are that David? The David, who tried to kill me?" This piece of information astounded me.

"Whoa, that was never my intention. I was never a killer. I wanted to show you the taste of real life back then. I'm sorry about what happened that day. I truly am." He clenched his

teeth.

"Real life! That's interesting because you managed to get me suspended for a week from school," I said.

"Let me clear up one thing... I was attracted to Islam then, but my sources of getting information were limited. I tried to read some books I found in the school library, but before I knew it, my father found out, and we went back to America just to keep me away from Islam. Who knew Allah would bring me back here right in front of you again."

"When did you realise that it was me?" I inquired.

"Remember the day when Dr. Sam called us together to his office and informed us about our community work? That was when I noticed it was you."

"That was only two months ago. You never saw me before that?"

"No, I'm afraid not," he said.

"I'm still confused how can you learn all about Islam to convert to it in less than two months?"

"I did not. That's the reason I'm in a hurry; I want my dear wife to teach me Islamic values and duties," he said still staring at the floor. Silence followed for five long minutes.

"I think I'm done here. Do you have any questions?" I inquired.

He just shook his head and kept on smiling widely.

39

ADAM HEARD the birds singing. He could smell the scent of moist soil. He moaned and pulled the pillow over his head to block the blinding light and the clamour of the rain. If only his head would explode and get it over with. At least the pillow seemed softer this morning, and it smelled nicer too; a fresh citrus scent that quickened his blood.

Rain? It doesn't sound like rain. He peeked out from under the pillow.

"Oh, not my room."

He sprang up on the bed, and turned his face around. His mind flashed back to last night's events, after grandmother gave him the diary. He retired to his room straight away and went to bed early to read. It was a small room upstairs. Unlike the others, this room had a window in it, facing the scenic views of the fields.

Dad reverted to Islam. Why didn't he tell me that? I'm sure he wasn't a Muslim then; I've never seen him pray the way they pray here. How can he ever be a Muslim? That's impossible. But, this diary says otherwise.

Frustrated, he got up and looked through the window. It was a fine morning. Bright blue sky with birds flying by, the lush green grassland, and the humming sound of water gushing down the drop was refreshing, yet Adam couldn't feel all that — stuck in the past.

"I've always thought knowing the truth would give my soul satisfaction. It seems like I am more devastated now than before," Adam said out loud.

Unintentionally, he took his father's notebook out of his coat pocket and flipped through the pages. Although, there was nothing new in it, the familiar words made him contented. He sighed and searched for his mother's diary. It was lying on the bed. To his surprise, he had read it all last night; the rest of the diary was empty. He went in search of his Grandmother.

"You said last night that this will tell me the past until my mother's death. I've read it all it ends way before that."

"My dear Adam, take a seat, and I'll tell you rest of it myself." She pointed to the sofa in front of her and continued, "The reason why this diary has nothing further than that was her death, Son. These were her last words she had ever written. She died the very next morning. I gather you know that you were born after her death. They saved you but couldn't save her."

Tears pooled into her eyes. Adam sat quietly for a while. His mind was exploding with thousands of questions and he was gathering the courage to ask.

"You want to know how they got married and what happened after that?"

"Yes, Grandmother," Adam replied.

"Well, first, call me Mamma. Everyone here calls me that, and, about their marriage, they married within a week's time, then Sarah moved in with David. They were happy, thrilled. David was a great man. He learned about Islam with her. She taught him how to pray and how to read The Quran. Then, one day, she came to us and gave us the happy news of her pregnancy. A few months later, my husband died of a heart attack. She took it hard. The doctors advised her bed rest, and it became harder than ever staying in the bed all day. So, David brought this diary and told her to write." She stopped for a moment to take in the grief and continued, "That day, her last day, she came and said that the doctors had told her it's a boy, so, she'd name him Adam the name of our Prophet Adam, the first man in this entire world. She said she wanted his son to do wonders for bringing back world peace.

We had a little party that day. Everyone was so happy. David made us laugh by making lame jokes out of nowhere. Then the next day I received a call from the police. They said she died from excessive bleeding through her neck, and the attacker was unconscious from David's blow with the chair. The only blissful news was that they saved the baby. David never said a word, not to the police, not even to me. I begged him to tell me the details, but he waited until the hospital cleared you and flew back to America without saying goodbye. He disappeared with you." It wore her from too much grief. Adam made his way towards her and sat by her feet, holding her hands quietly, mystified with the fact he couldn't get any further information about what had happened that night.

Dad, why didn't you tell me anything? I was your son, only son. He knew that no one could answer his queries now.

"Assalamualaikum, how was your first night here?" Mujahid entered the library.

"Well, it was fine," replied Adam softly.

"Khadim has requested me to bring you both to breakfast," Mujahid informed.

"Breakfast... let's go," said Mamma while wiping her tears away.

40

BEWITCHED BY the surroundings outside the fort, Adam stood at the front door. The waterfall on his right looked like a sheet of blue velour as it swished down, and its edged were hemmed with whipped white lines. The weather was perfect, the wind was blowing fiercely with a mixture of honey-sweet smell of the flowers nearby and the damp soil. The terraces of the vegetation; the levels on the steep platform on his left, looked like steps with thick green carpets.

"Let's start our tour now," Mujahid suggested.

"Yes, that would be great." Adam had agreed to have a tour after the breakfast; he badly wanted to divert his thoughts.

"I'm still surprised; how come a cliff like this could be in the middle of hot dry mountains? And the temperature, it's awesome. This place is so enchanting, the beauty beyond any limits. It's amazing," Adam wondered out loud.

"It sure is," said Mujahid, "These terraces are the product of Mamma's hard work. Khadim helped her a lot. She says that she doesn't need the world's help to live. She usually grows necessary vegetables here, plus, there are some cattle at the back of the new construction."

"This white hut at the front is the new construction you're talking about, right?"

"Well, yes, that's the newest one. It was constructed when Mamma came here to live. She wanted a clear view of the falls. As you can see, there are large wooden windows on each side," informed Mujahid.

"This door, is it a new construction?" Asked Adam.

"No. It was the front door of the old construction," Mujahid answered.

"What about the old fort? We could start a tour of that now," suggested Adam.

"Let's go inside then."

They crossed the narrow lobby and into the square room before the dining hall.

"This was the old fort's front lobby. To our right, as you've been there, is the dining hall. They constructed this hall, the library, and Mamma's room in front of the library long after the first build. About a hundred years ago, the British Empire built it for their personal use."

"How did it end up with Mamma, then?"

"Well, when they left South Asia, Mamma claimed this place as she was the descendent of the real owner. Fortunately, she had no problems. It's been almost three decades since she came back from Scotland," Mujahid explained as they walked into the kitchen on the far side of the front lobby.

"This kitchen was part of the old construction. It's over a thousand years old. See the walls; these are made of carved stones. Here are some old stone vessels used for cooking."

For Adam, the stoves made from carved stone were fascinating. They went out to the room that connected the kitchen and the library.

"Where do these doors go," inquired Adam, pointing towards the three small doors in a row, right under the front wall of the kitchen.

"These are old prison rooms, moreover dungeons. They go right under the kitchen, and they made them here because they wanted their prisoners to suffer the heat coming from the kitchen stoves," Mujahid added as he started climbing the stairs. "Let's go upstairs now."

The lobby to their right led them to the three adjacent rooms. The first one, Mujahid's, and the one on the far side was Adam's.

"What about this bathroom? Is it old construction too?"

"No, of course not. The British people made them

one here on the first floor and the other downstairs," Mujahid replied.

On their left, a door led them to the terrace. It was almost mid-day then. The sun shone brightly up on top. Adam stood by the terrace wall. The view was overwhelming. The top of the cliff in front was a flat bed, and the crest of the waterfall was on his right. The sound of the gushing water was then rumbling loudly over the rocks.

Standing there at the edge of the roof, he saw someone down the path towards the front door. Adam blinked twice to clear if his eyes were deceiving him. The light pink coat and the flower-patterned scarf – she was standing there with her bag by her side. He was so numb that he couldn't even utter a single word.

"Wait, who's that?" Mujahid said, as soon as he reached the edge, "I'm going downstairs. There can't be just anyone wandering about. She must be here to meet Mamma," Mujahid added as he walked out.

41

FLUSTERED BY the sight her eyes witnessed, Iman didn't blink, as she expected none other than her Grandmother's sister, Mamma, who lived alone, far away from the world. The reason why she travelled all the way from Lahore was to get away from her community; to get away from men. Yet, there she was standing at the front door welcomed by a man. Though this man was soft, placid, and humble, she could tell all that from his face, the soft lines and the very humble smile he wore made her feel at home. He was standing by the door asking a simple question which she was gathering the courage to answer but it seemed like the words refused to come out.

"Ma'am, please come inside. I'll tell Mamma that you are here."

The moment she heard those words, she hurried inside and followed him to the library, which made her forget about her worries. Lost in the view of the bookshelves filled with books at each corner. Her dream place.

"Assalamualaikum my child." She turned and saw Mamma standing by the door.

"Wàlikumassallam, Mamma, I am..."

Before she could finish her words, Mamma replied as she took her seat, "Iman, the granddaughter of my sister; I can surely see the resemblance, my child."

"Yes, Mamma," Iman whispered.

"Come here, I want to hug you." Mamma stretched out her arms, Iman wasted no time and compiled. "Ah, I can smell the scent of her. She was just like you when she was young. So thin and tall." Mamma hugged her tighter.

"Mamma, would you let me stay here? I'm tired. I want a break from the life out there," said Iman.

"My pleasure, my child. That was the reason I came here a long time ago. You are most welcome, but there's one thing, I have a visitor these days, my grandson Adam. You will have to tolerate him," said Mamma.

"Well, I won't have any problems, he seems to be a nice guy," replied Iman.

"Have you met him already?" Mamma inquired.

"Yes, he opened the door for me."

"No, my child, you are mistaken; that was Mujahid, he lives here with me. He's more like my son. The Grandson I'm talking about is Adam who's visiting me from America. He's an American." Iman opened her mouth in astonishment, but before she could bring out the words, Mamma continued, "You can stay with me. My room is large enough, and we have a spare room upstairs, but the boys are staying on each of the sides of that room. You don't have any problems staying with me. Do you?"

"No, not all. I would be happier. I'm not used to living alone in a separate room. I hope it won't be the other way around for you, though," Iman said.

"No, no, my child, I will be fine. Maybe it's time I have somebody by my side. I'm having difficulty with walking these days, and the bathroom is on the far side of the floor." Mamma smiled and said, "I think you should go get some rest before lunch; we'll have our lunch in the library. I'll tell Khadim to arrange for that," Mamma suggested.

"Yes, that would be great. Oh, I forgot to give this to you. It's the letter from my mother," Iman handed her the letter and went into the room.

It was a huge rectangular room exactly the size of the library just opposite it. The instant she entered the room she felt cosy and warm as if she was on a bed of roses. There was a bed by one of the large windows and a couch on the other. Once she made herself comfortable on the couch, she closed her eyes, remembering that day. The hardest day she had ever lived.

When they entered the room that day, a small square room that had only a foot's space in between the door and the desk, she saw her zip-lock bag still intact, placed up front on the table. Yet the frightening sight was the man behind the desk; Ahaan, who was gathering his stuff. As soon as he sat his eyes on them he picked up his pistol, rushed towards Iman, and placing it over her head, he said, "You think you both can run away? I guess I have to end this story once and for all. Pity that I didn't praise your beauty."

"Don't! You're not gonna do that," Ahmed said. Within a second he kicked Ahaan's pistol, which made a screeching sound of metal sliding down towards the door, while he grabbed Iman's hand and dragged her out of Ahaan's reach. But before he could do more, Ahaan twisted back to his table and picked up another pistol from his drawer, and wasting no time he pressed the trigger; its loud sound filled the air. Ahmed started bleeding. Iman pooled her hands under his falling body. "Please don't go," she said.

The radio beeped and cracked, bringing back broken words of someone from the other side. "Boss, hurry. The helicopter is ready."

"I wish you had more time, but dear, you need to come with me."

Ahaan's words spread energy through Ahmed's entire body. Before Ahaan could grab her hand, he rained blows onto him, as if he meant to smash him into the earth. Turning towards Iman he said, "Run! Take your bag and run."

She stood there, thunderstruck with the sudden action. Ahaan began his set of blows focusing on the wound. He bashed onto Ahmed, the only word that filled the air was 'run'. She slowly neared the table, grabbed the bag and turned around, but she knew she had to do something; she couldn't possibly leave her husband there. Her eyes landed on shiny metal. The deadly weapon. She rushed towards it. Without thinking, she grabbed the gun and pressed the trigger three times with her eyes closed.

Bang — bang — bang.

When she opened her eyes again, she found the lifeless body of Ahaan up on the top of Ahmed. Blood was rushing out.

"Ya—Allah, are you okay?" She threw the gun and pushed Ahaan's body away from her husband, only to find him cold as ice.

Iman heard a knock at the door. "Yes, who is it?"

"Madam, your lunch is served; please come to the library," said Khadim.

"Okay, I'll be there in a minute," said Iman as she stood up and headed towards the door.

42

"SHE'S NOT eating with us? What kind of guest is she? Is she a princess or something?" Adam stormed out those questions soon after he learnt that Iman was a guest and that she would have her lunch with Mamma in the library.

"Well, Adam, actually in the values we follow, the Islamic values that is, each woman is a princess, so we respect them and their hijab," replied Mujahid.

"So, does she wear the hijab in front of every man, like she won't take it off even when she is with her father?" Adam grinned.

"No, not in front of her family," said Mujahid.

"Oh," replied Adam in a low voice, remembering his mother's words.

Silence continued for five long minutes. How did his father find his values vague in just a month's time, and why would a person leave those newly discovered ideologies and spend half of his life as a non-believer of God? There should be a reason. The more Adam went into the how's and the why's, the more desperate he grew to know – but that urge for knowledge raised another how. How could he ever find out about his father's side of story?

"Adam, please eat your lunch, it's getting cold." Mujahid dragged him back to the present.

"What's this dish called? It's delicious." Adam tried to sound interested but his voice mumbled.

"Well, it's a dish from Afghanistan. It's called Kabuli Palau. Khadim learned this dish from his Afghani friend," answered Mujahid.

"Hmm."

"After lunch, if you are not tired, we could have a tour of the falls," suggested Mujahid.

"Yes, that would be fine. I think I need fresh air." Adam jerked his head in the affirmative.

"I think you should get a little rest first. You can go out after Asar prayer; the atmosphere is more refreshing by then," suggested Khadim.

"Okay. We'll go after Asar then," said Mujahid.

"And when exactly is this Asar prayer time?" inquired Adam with a slight sneer on his face.

"These days it's nearly four o'clock," Mujahid smiled.

"Okay, two hours from now. I'll definitely get

some rest till then," Adam said and excused himself to his room upstairs.

"I will not think about anything now. Just close your eyes and get some rest," Adam ordered himself. But instead of closing his eyes, he bounced up and stood by the window, watching the green fields and the cattle, the goats with thick long hair, huge round antlers, and some hens.

"I can't stay here like this," he said to himself and headed out.

43

MAX SAT there on his bunk, smiling. His ears rang with the loud sound of a fire alarm, and his nostrils, for the first time in his prison life, picked the pungent smell of burning clothes. Something other than the litter inside his cell. His smile faded as that burning smell reminded him of yet another miserable day of his life and the day a few years before that one.

At first, he was happy that he would meet Sarah after so many years. He made sure he wore nice clean clothes that his grandfather brought for the Christmas party, the cologne he had stolen from his late father's drawer, and the shoes he had polished, spending two hours straight.

But then everything changed when he said hello and asked her if she could sit with him, and Sarah replied, "I am sorry; I cannot be friends with you anymore. I am a grown-up Muslim girl now, and we have limitations. I will be here for whatever you need of me, as long as it's about studies, but other than that we cannot spend time together chatting like we used to do when we were kids."

For Max, his whole life turned upside down. He had but one hope. The hope of being friends with her again. The hope of forgetting his life at home and spending the school hours in fairy tales. The beautiful memories of her kept him alive after he pushed his father and the times when his grandfather turned even worse than his own son. They were only six years old when she left, but he remembered each day spent with her. The day when they played hide and seek, the day when she read stories and stories to him, and the pet day when she brought a pet for him too as he had none of his own.

He had everything at stake for the past few years, and this was what he got. Furious with the reply, he ran, circling round and round the stadium.

His wishes came true in the form of a boy who grabbed his arm and said, "If you are running because they said you can't be friends with them, then I am here, I am new and they said that to me too. Really, we should stick together and give them a lesson. Tell them we are better and they are but some puppet."

Blood rushed through his eyes every time he relived that day. He felt the heat, and tightened both of his fists. That day, he gave up the tiniest hope left inside him, and promised himself to give them what they deserved, but then he would always smile while recalling the outcome; he had been lucky enough to fulfil his promise twice, and he would surely be lucky enough to finish what he had started. And for him, that was the only purpose left.

44

THAT DAY, after the alarm went off, they took almost an hour to transfer Max to the auditorium with the rest of the prisoners, but they sent Rocky to the high security cell, away from the rest. Max took this opportunity and deliberately sit beside Dexter.

"So, what is your specialty other than killing your own father?"

"Well, since I've heard that you're about to get released I will tell you. Maybe you'll need my services. I make fake IDs and passports."

"You are in prison, you know that? How can I take advantage of your services now?"

"I will connect you with my friend, he will make them for you, and I'll get my cut here. That's how."

"Oh, then I would avail your services as soon as I am released. I have an unfinished job and I need to travel to America for that. They won't let me enter with my current status."

"That's great, go to the coffee shop named 'Coffee 77', and ask for Dublin Backster. Tell him I've sent you and he will help you in whatever you need him for. But these things cost a lot. Do you have money for it?"

"Yes, I do. I have been saving a lot from the day I had stepped here I knew I would need it if I want my unfinished job done as soon as I am out."

"Be careful though. They keep an eye on you once you're out; at least for a year or two."

"Yes, I am not planning to travel until two years. Need to figure out my plan and find my target."

"Hmm! We use original ID's rented by the residents so you won't get any trouble," Dexter whispered.

"Wonderful."

SHE SAT there behind the falls, hidden from the harsh rays of the sun, her hands placed on her face. No matter how much she tried, she couldn't get rid of the memories of that day – getting out of that dreadful building was one thing, and then she had to reach the airport on time.

"It was some unseen force which helped me do what I did. I really can't believe it myself," she whispered, remembering every moment like a nightmare. When she rushed out of the secret door behind the cabinet which led her to the adjacent building, she heard a police officer repeating the same phrase over his radio again and again. "We have surrounded the building. Please surrender and come out. You have five minutes."

"If I hadn't taken the number of that old lady from the street, I wouldn't have been able to get to the airport, let alone change my clothes and take a small bag to deceive the customs," she whispered, "Ah! It feels like a nightmare, a terrible nightmare. Oh God! I felt so relieved that my mother sensed my problems without getting any words out of me. Thank God that she sent me here before I could face anyone else from the family."

46

ADAM AMBLED towards the fall. The unusual humming sound vibrated in his ears; it sounded like a swarm of bees. Then, the buzzing transferred to the rock beneath his feet. It travelled through his body and he felt a tingle that ran up to his fingertips. He rounded the corner and the source of the sound revealed itself. The sound increased into growling and rumbling when he moved closer to the edge where he could see the base of the falls. He looked up to have a clear view of its crest and witnessed that the water fused itself into distant threads of watery fabric which looked like a sheet of silver tear tracks on the wrinkled faces of the rocks.

Then, he saw the same flower-patterned scarf and the same pink coat filtering right through the fall. She was sitting on the rock. His spectacular vision blurred out by the water. Her head was down to her knees, and her hands were crossing through them.

She stood up and walked past the waterfall; standing right in front of him, staring as if she had seen a ghost.

"What are you doing here?" she inquired in a harsh tone.

"I'm here to admire the beauty," Adam replied with a slight grin on his face.

"I mean, what are you doing here? Like here, at this place. Did you follow me?"

"Follow you? Are you insane? Why would I follow you?" Adam said, surprised by her statement.

"What's the big deal? Did I miss something?" inquired Mujahid from behind.

"Her highness thinks I came here by following her," Adam smirked.

"Well, Iman Behan, this is Mamma's Grandson, Adam. And Adam, this is Miss Iman, our guest," Mujahid said with a smile twisting across his face.

"Oh, I'm sorry." As soon as Iman said those words she flew back to the fort with lightning speed.

"Oh my! Did she say she was sorry?" Adam said and walked towards the rock where she had been sitting. The water falling right in front of his eyes presented a perfect example of bewitching scenery. Adding to the scene were the thundering sounds of falling water. Mujahid followed him and sat by his side. Adam turned towards Mujahid and said, "Why would a girl like her come to such a place? I mean, this is a remote area. There's almost nothing here like

Internet or even a mobile phone service."

"Well, I don't know her real purpose, but maybe she's just visiting because this place is beautiful. Some people actually travel to admire."

"Maybe." Adam quietly sat there for a minute then he said, "So what do you think – is there someone who created all these wonderful places?"

"In my opinion, it's none other than Allah Subhana Tàlla. He's the one and only Supreme Being of the entire universe; the One who has no family and no siblings."

"Why would your Allah create this world? Surely we aren't worth all this. Are we? We create chaos and fight with each other. Why would He still be so grateful to let us be?" Adam asked.

"Well, we don't know the half of it. Only the part we know is, he created this world to test us. It's an examination hall for us. The ones, who'll pass will go to Jannah, and the ones who fail will be thrown into hell."

"You know, I've never been through this phase before ever in my life, till now. I hadn't thought about anything beyond myself, but this place is making me think in a way I always hated. I don't really know what's happening to me. It feels like I knew it all but I don't. It's funny that when I made my decision to come, my friend told me to be careful because Muslims are magicians; they change you without even giving a hint. Now, when I'm experiencing your company myself, it feels different. Enchanting and amazing. I really want to believe every word of yours," Adam said.

SHE WENT into the library to hide herself under a book. She stared at the huge shelves trying to find the courage to pick a book.

"You are back already? It's not Asar time yet, and they won't be out until four o'clock," Mamma said while taking her seat beside Iman.

"It appears they're out before they said they would, so I came back. Mamma, I was wondering how your grandson could be an American. That man is nothing close to any Pakistani."

"Well, you aren't looking closely. He's more like me, only his style of speaking and his dress say otherwise," replied Mamma.

"He called me your highness. I didn't get it, why would he call me that?"

"Hmm, your highness — interesting," Mamma grinned.

"And he never said Assalamualaikum too, is he not a Muslim? Didn't your daughter marry a Muslim guy?"

"No, he's not a Muslim; it appears that his father had brought him up without the knowledge of the existence of Allah. It's really strange to me. His father was a Muslim when he left Scotland with him back then. Why would he do such a thing? Islam is a beautiful Deen; a complete one. Once you enter it, you never leave its ways. Ah, we can't find out his side of the story, now that he's dead," Mamma sighed.

"He must be a born Muslim, then?" asked Iman.

"Yes, my dear, I myself saw David giving the Adhan in his ears there in the hospital."

"I hope Allah will show him the righteous path to Jannah. Insha-Allah," Iman whispered, looking at the books and making the face of a kid who has seen a roomful of candies.

"You can read any book you want; my collections are mostly old historical books. There in the left shelf you'll find all the historical fiction. I've marked all the shelves," Mamma mentioned.

"Yes, Mamma, I would love to. In fact, I was about to ask you if I can read these books."

"Sure, Baita. You don't need any permission."

Iman went to the bookshelf to her left and found more books than she could ever wish to read. As her mouth opened with astonishment she said, "Oh, how lovely all these books are. I have always wanted to read. I can't choose which one to read first. Mamma, can you suggest?"

"Well, what kind of books do you like?"

"I like suspense and thriller."

"Hmm, very interesting. I expected that you would say a love story, though."

"Normally, I would read one, but nowadays I would rather be far away."

"What do you say about Sherlock Holmes, then? I have some of the original magazines that printed his series back then."

"Seriously? That's awesome."

"Fourth row, second column on your left. There is a thick binder marked SH magazines."

Iman took the book out of the shelves and placed herself near Mamma.

"This is amazing. This one is dated 1881. How could it possibly end up here?"

"The British left most of these books here. I don't know what happened; they took all their stuff from the rest of Pakistan, but this place was an exception. They never even touched it. When I first came here there was a book lying on this very sofa as if somebody had run away in a hurry leaving all the things behind. Nobody really knows what happened here as this place's real owners were my ancestors, so

I reclaimed it back in 1974. It hadn't been discovered until then by any of the locals here. By the way, I never asked how you happened to come here without any help. That's almost impossible. This place doesn't even exist in Google maps," Mamma ended with an inquiry Iman was waiting to answer.

"Ah! Mamma, my mother had the number of the driver who used to deliver you the gifts my mother sent you every now and then. Actually, Mama said she'd send you the request first, but I was desperate to get away."

"Yes, I've read your mother's letter. I'm happy that I'm being helpful to anyone. This place is wonderful for getting away from the busy life of elsewhere."

"I loved this place the minute I stepped on the platform. The fall, the fields, and the old fort... everything is incredibly marvellous."

"Have you visited the upper floor yet? Now is the best time to do it, you know; the boys are out."

"Maybe. I hope they don't come back before I'm done."

"I'll keep an eye on them and send Khadim to tell you."

"Okay." Iman got up, crossed the lobby and climbed up the stairs to the terrace.

The instant she laid her eyes on the scenery she started praising Allah. The sun was almost down by then; the purple and pink sky with orange beams of the sun simmering from beneath the cliff's bed together with the humming sound of water flowing made the scenery more divine.

48

ADAM WAS still sitting on that very stone, lost in thought, thinking about the cause of the existence of this world, and watching Mujahid offer his Maghrib prayer near the fall. His body was fuming from behind by the fading light of the Sun; the purple, pink and orange colours mixing and filtering through Mujahid's torso. It was as if he was seeing the world with entirely new eyes.

Is there really some kind of God that created all this? There must be someone or something that is responsible for creating this beauty. Then, is it really the One Mujahid's talking about? What does he call Him, oh yes, Allah? Is He really the One?

"What do you think about having a camp fire here?" said Mujahid while getting up.

"I think I would love to stay near the falls as much as I can. So, yes, that would be wonderful."

"I'll go and bring some wood and a matchbox. You can come with me if you want."

"I'll be fine here. Loving the sunset; it's magical," Adam praised.

"Okay! I'll be back soon."

Adam sat there, waiting for Mujahid to return. These were the times when he would unknowingly bring his father's handbook out from his pocket and begin flipping through the familiar pages. He felt something strange that day as he took the handbook out while holding it with his left hand and grabbing the cover from the other side. It was thicker than the front side he usually held. He instantly compared the two sides. There were pages hidden in the cover flap at the back of the book. Lots of them.

How could he miss such a thing?

He had flipped the very handbook thousands of times before. He peeked inside those pages and found the one thing he was desperate to read.

A letter addressed to him; a letter from his beloved father to his only son.

49

MY DEAR *Adam, How are you, Son? I hope you find this letter in the best health. I'm writing this to answer each and every question you asked about your Mother and our life. If you're wondering why didn't I tell you anything before, I must clarify that I didn't have any courage then; I couldn't possibly face you after what I had done to you. When your mother died, I got so devastated by the life I was living, that I left it and came back to my previous ways with a bitter heart towards our creator. At first, I was happy with my actions – bringing you up as a non-believer of God. Then, slowly and gradually, my grief subsided and I felt hollow. The failure, suffering and remorse made me walk on thorns.*

Especially when I saw you becoming the most self-centred person one could ever be, I tried several times to gather the courage to give you the right knowledge, to turn you towards the right path. By then I was late. Too late. How could I ever tell you about my mistakes? Not face to face. What a stupid and spiteful person I was to leave the most enchanting and wonderful belief there is in this whole world.

Maybe, just maybe, someday you'll find this letter and get your answers from it. Hopefully, you'll also find the right path from it. God always provides ways to choose good over bad in this world. It's upon us to take it or not.

I first met your mother when I was in my seventh grade. My father moved our family to Stirling, Scotland, because of his work and stuff. I'd never seen a Muslim girl in my life before. Also, a girl wearing hijab was new to me.

I always got what I wanted back then. Girls tended to bounce up and down near me. I'm not at all exaggerating. They all did. But not her; she was different. Quiet and calm, yet, brilliant in her studies. Her modesty bothered me. I always wondered why a girl would wear that kind of covered clothing. It was inviting, very inviting, as if calling for attention; it separated her from the rest of the class. She never talked to any of the school boys the way the rest of the girls did; she spoke only important school stuff with clear bitterness in her voice. Bitter, yet sweet. Hard ,yet soft. I tried to talk to her several times, but she never listened to anything other than the talk about studies. I scolded her and called her names. She would just bear them with a soft smile and walk away. I even tried to ask her why she wore that thing over her head. She replied with two words and fled into the class.

"For Allah."

Devastated by her reply I searched for books to get my answers. I was in my middle grade then. I didn't have any access to the right kind of books, only the books in our school library, and they did not satisfy me. So, I started questioning people.

People like my father and mother or our priest.

One day, my best friend Max and I made a promise to ourselves to break her from her little world. To tell her that she's not some princess or anything. My objective was to let her feel the freedom. Freedom from that covered life. I seriously thought that the covering and the stiff behaviour was forced by her parents, and from inside, she'd love to get out and live free.

Max was desperate to show her the bold life she could have lived. He was more into showing the world that nobody should force anyone into living their lives as they want them to. Maybe it was because he had problems with his family; his father died when he was young and his grandfather was a nightmare who forced him to do many things in his life which he otherwise wouldn't do. His upbringing was dark and enforced. He had often been beaten up by his grandfather for little things. I honestly didn't know back then about his extreme ideas or I would have stopped him beforehand, and I regret that from the bottom of my heart. If only I knew what was coming. If only I could change the past now. I should have at least tried to make him feel differently, but I didn't have any clue of his beliefs back then.

It was a Saturday. We were at the school for some extra class. The rest of the school was off, and there were few of us working in the lab. We waited for her to go towards the library storeroom where she used to pray.

That day, we followed her and went inside. She was praying, standing on a rug silently looking down with crossed hands. I was mesmerized by the mere sight of her. Before I knew it Max went over to her and grabbed her scarf off of her head. Within a second he set it on fire and started yelling, 'Run, David, run."

I glanced at her. She was miserable, covering her face with her hands. I don't know what made me do what I did that day but I ran like Max told me to and never looked back.

I ran and ran until I reached my room. The instant my mind processed what just happened, I became worried — worried about her.

That night, my father came to me and told me that we were going back to America by Monday morning's flight. I asked him why so suddenly, but he didn't reply. I knew for sure that they'd called him about that day, but he never said a word about it.

I became so desperate that I asked permission on Sunday to visit my friend Max to say goodbye, but my father said no. We flew back to America without even knowing what happened to her. Life became miserable. I used to have nightmares of her burning and screaming. It took me almost two years to feel normal. I didn't forget her at all; instead, I got accustomed to those nightmares.

50

"I'VE BROUGHT the wood for the camp fire," Mujahid said while arranging the logs.

"I'm amazed. Have you ever found the knowledge you're dying for, hidden all along in plain sight and wondered how could you miss such a thing?" Adam showed Mujahid the hidden pages from afar.

"Well, Adam, Allah knows the best time to reveal knowledge. Maybe it's Allah's wish to let you know now rather than before." Mujahid began working on the fire.

"Yes, maybe because if I had found his letter before, I would've become angry. Now, after knowing my mother's side of the story, I'm fine."

"Do you want to read that in peace? I could go back to Mamma if you want?"

"No, please sit here with me. We'll read it together. I need someone to be with me right now," Adam said, surprised by the words that fell out of his mouth.

They settled down near the fire and Adam started reading the rest of the letter, after briefly telling Mujahid about the part he had just read.

51

L ATER, MY *father told me, when he was on his deathbed, that he did all that to protect my faith. I asked him whether he knew what had happened to her. He said she was fine. They gave her a week's detention for going into the storeroom without permission. I was shocked. Upon further questioning, he told me that they left my involvement in the dark to protect the school's image.*

After that, I became more desperate to know the truth about Islam. I started researching it. Then I got this scholarship at the University of Stirling for medicine. The moment I walked into Stirling, my premium objective was to find her and see if she was fine. I knew she had always vowed to become a doctor someday, and I knew how much she loved Stirling University. I waited. It took me more than a year, but there came a day when I finally saw her. She was happy as she got the scholarship for the medical school that year. I never made any move to talk to her, just used to pass by her and observe. Even when your mother asked after I'd proposed her when I actually realized who she was, I didn't have the courage to tell her much. I sometimes feel that I'm a coward in these matters. I can't confess. I can't say sorry. However, I did try to look after her without her knowledge. Then, after I accepted Islam, I went straight to her father and asked for her hand in marriage.

We got married in about a week's time. She moved in with me, and everything was perfect. I used to learn about Islam from her: how to read and understand the Qur'an, and how to pray. She was a very good teacher, you know. I loved every minute I spent with her. Only Allah knows better, but those lovely moments didn't last long. She got pregnant with you soon after our marriage. What we didn't know then was that misfortune was just round the corner.

I can't forget that day. It was the longest day in my life. The day it all happened and changed my life once and for all. We were celebrating her seven months pregnancy and they told us that it was a boy. She was happy. She made an exquisite dinner that day. We had it early, and when we were about to retire to bed, the worst nightmare came into our life.

He came back. Out of the blue, Max stood by our bed with a dagger in his hands. He grabbed her and ordered me to keep still. I tried the telephone despite his warnings, but it was dead. Then, I felt something hard hit me on the head, and everything went blurry. When I woke up, I found myself tied to a chair right in front of her. She was on the bed lying flat with her hands and legs tied. He was standing next to her, wiping her tears out with a sympathetic smile, telling her to stop crying as if he was really concerned about her. He was a psycho with a dagger in his hands. I tried to shout, but my mouth was duct-taped. Although I could hear her cries, I couldn't do anything. I felt useless. She was shouting and screaming. She was in agony and I felt it too. The only question was, why was he doing it? Why was he hurting her? Then, his eyes met mine and he advanced towards me.

"You. You are the one responsible for all of this. You broke your promise. Do you remember? We promised back then to let her feel the freedom, and you, instead of keeping your promise, you became one of them. The ones who order people to live the way they want them to. You became a monster yourself. It's Sarah, isn't it? She has some kind of magic. The magic she used when we were kids ourselves. The words she used when she promised me; she said she'd be my friend forever, didn't you?" Max twisted his face towards her and said, "I'm going to show you what happens when people break promises, and I am going to keep mine. The promise I made with you to show the world the right ways of living. To tell them that everyone needs the freedom to live. I am going to give her the freedom; freedom from you, freedom from her forced faith, an eternal freedom."

"Please, please, don't do this. I'll do whatever you say, but I have a child, and I want him to live a long life. Please have mercy," Sarah pleaded. But he was desperate. He said he didn't want anyone to suffer like he had. He told us that he would make sure this little one never saw the bitterness of the world. I was hoping that maybe somebody passing by would hear her screams and call the police. Then it happened. The very thing I was afraid of. He left my side and went straight to her, placing his knife at her neck. I don't know what happened next. Time slowed down and sped up at the same time. I heard police sirens in the background. I felt like the most helpless person in whole wide world. The site of the splashed blood made me jump up with the chair. I turned around and hit the back of his head with the legs of the chair. In a split second, he was lying still on the floor. I took matters in my hand, but I was late. Too late. The paramedics came rushing in and started working on her.

My child! Do you know? I didn't even get the chance to say goodbye; to tell her that I loved her the most and that I loved her more than anything in the world. She was uttering the words one should be, the Kalimah — praising Allah.

I never said a word to anyone. This is the first time I've ever admitting that I knew the killer. I don't know why I did that, but I didn't have any words to explain all this back then. I couldn't possibly tell the whole story at that time when I was so grieved and depressed. When they told me that they had saved you, I made a promise to myself that I would take you away, away from all this. To a place where you'd be safe, and I would never come back, never make contact with these people again. So, I took you and flew back to America. Now, I regret my actions, but you must understand that those actions were the result of my sorrow, my grief, and my despair.

Please, I beg you to visit your only family left, your grandmother. She lives in Pakistan now. She had contacted me several times. At first, I didn't want you to meet her, but afterwards, I didn't have the courage to tell you anything. I'm adding her contact details on the back. Please, if you want to know anything about your mother or the right way of living, it's there, with her. Meet your grandmother and ask her. Believe everything she says. She's the most amazing woman I've ever met. She is your family. She has the right knowledge about the way we should spend our time in this world.

One last thing I want you know is that I'm a Muslim. I was and I am. I left the path for a few years, but couldn't find peace. Without my beliefs, I was empty. After I realized that, I *started following the ways Allah has told us to follow, again. For you, I was too late. I tried to tell you, to lead you to the path, but you never listened to any of it.*

GO VISIT HER.

That's my last wish.

From your loving Father.

52

"MY MOTHER, she died right in front of him. He was there. How could he even live after all that? It explains a lot. You know my father in his last days, he used to connect every little happening with the existence of God, explaining our purpose for living in a way that I always got frustrated and distressed by it. Every time he brought up the subject I would get up and leave. I never listened to any of his words then. He had become so soft and placid that he even tried to take me to one of those places... what do you call the place you pray in?"

"Masjid," Mujahid muttered.

"Yes, Masjid. I never went in. I was like, maybe, because of his bad health he's seeking forgiveness from every place of worship. I was sure that I wasn't going to die anytime soon, so why would I go inside those places. If he's worried about his life hereafter, he should go, not me. Besides, I never believed in any such stuff then," Adam paused and processed his own words. Does he really believe in all this now? Is there a God and an afterlife?

"So, you have the book. What do you call it? Yes — the Qur'an. Do you have it right now? I want to read it."

"I sure do. Actually, I've brought a copy of English translation for you. I was hoping you would ask for one," Mujahid produced a small square Qur'an from his pocket and handed it to him.

Adam flipped some pages and started reading. The first thing he noticed was the language, deep and warm. Tactful, with grace. Un-put-down-able and very inviting.

"We created man from an essence of clay, then We placed him as a drop of fluid in a safe place, then We developed that drop into a clinging form, and We developed that form into a lump of flesh, and We developed that lump into bones, and clothed the bones with flesh. Then we brought him into being as a new creation—glory be to God, the best of creators—after this you shall surely die. Then you will be raised up again on the Resurrection Day," Adam read a verse out loud.

"This book — it's all the words of God, right? Not a word by any human?"

"No, it's not; only Allah's words. Isn't it wonderful? Allah has mentioned things over fourteen hundred years ago that were recently proven by science," Mujahid said those words and became silent again. The words that could make anyone's heart melt.

After a long time quietly observing Adam reading, Mujahid broke the silence again.

"It's getting late. I think we should go inside," he said while glancing at his watch. It was past midnight. Adam looked around and was astonished to see the sky filled with stars and streaks of coloured beams. Stars winked at him from the endless arch of black void. In places, they were birthstone-blue and beautiful, all the glitter in their heavenly finery. The ones furthest away, almost outside the span of human comprehension, were like flashing pinpricks in a veil of darkness. They had a faint, silver tint. All of them were beacons of hope for his lost soul. The waterfall, looked like bright white threads that sparkled uneasily in the dim light and shimmered like the ghostly blood drops of a phantom.

53

"MAMMA, I was wondering, you seem to be a practicing Muslim. How did you end up here?" asked Iman as she took the place by her side.

"Well, Baita, I was a normal, liberal person. It was my husband; he taught me many things about Islam."

"So how did you two get married. He was a Scottish, right?"

"Not exactly, his roots came from Pakistan too. He was born there, sure, and lived in Scotland all of his life. I used to work in his mother's bakery when I was graduating from the university in Stirling," Mamma replied.

"Yes, Nani Ammi told me about how you struggled hard to get that scholarship and to convince your father to let you go. You were the first one in the family who had the courage to even try such things,"

Iman added.

"Father let her marry soon after her intermediate examination only to make sure she didn't follow my footsteps. It was good for her, though. She wasn't the kind who could bear all the hardships I suffered. Studying abroad was harder than I thought it would be."

"Exactly, like marrying abroad was harder for me. I mean everyone told me I was lucky to find a match so handsome and all, but I never knew it's not the charm that matters. The most important thing was his personality, his real self. Is he soft? Does he understand? Is he a good guy? What are his beliefs?" Iman paused to wipe the tears off.

"Sure, my child. I know it wasn't at all your fault. In fact, it's nobody's fault. It's the way things are meant to be. Look at the bright side. If you hadn't had that past, would you have come here and met me? This place is magical, isn't it?"

"Ah, it sure is. I felt relieved the moment I stepped into this place."

Iman wanted to cry, she needed a shoulder who would understand her grief, who would listen to her story. She had to tell somebody what she had done, but before she could gather the courage to ask, she heard footsteps coming from behind her. She turned around and saw Adam standing by the doorway with the Book in his hands; the very Book that gave her comfort every time she read it.

"I want to talk to you Mamma," Adam's words made Iman stand up, and she ran past him, straight to the next room and locked herself in.

"What's her problem? Couldn't she stay where she was? Why can't she behave like a normal person? Are they all like this, running and hiding?"

"Well, my child, her loving husband died recently, and she came back home; she's disturbed about it. She needs time to heal."

"Oh, that is awful, I guess."

"Yes! It sure is. So what exactly do you want to talk about?" she added after a while.

"I wanted you to read my father's letter. I've found them in his planner. It was there the whole time and I didn't have a clue." He handed her the book, pointing out the pages he wanted her to read, she instantly started reading.

"That concludes all the missing pieces, explaining a lot of your father's actions," Mamma said after finishing the letter. Her eyes were filled with tears. For the first time, Adam saw her weak and distressed.

Adam made his way towards her, sat by her lap, putting his head down, he whispered the words that fulfilled her, "Mamma, I want to learn about Islam."

$$54$$

THOSE DARK black eyes were destined to be filled with tears, and that was the only belief that stayed inside Iman for the past six months. They say time would heal any misery, but for Iman time made it all worse. Her dreams turned into nightmares. The fact that she hadn't been able to open up to anyone not even Mamma, was making it harder.

"Mamma, I need to cry. I need to tell someone. Would you listen to me?" she finally said one cold afternoon. They sat by the fireplace, both of them reading books. One could say Iman was only pretending to read because those were the days she couldn't focus. Not even reading books helped her.

"Yes, my child, I am all ears. Spill whatever you've kept inside," Mamma placed her book on her lap and patted her shoulder.

"I killed a man before I ran back to Pakistan," she

said bluntly and started crying. Then she continued, "He was my husband's boss who killed my husband and he kidnapped us both for a week. We were trapped inside his building. I don't know what happened. It all happened so fast. Thankfully, I had the number to call, otherwise I would have stuck there. And the police — I dream about them;finding me and taking me to prison. It was self-defence Mamma. I swear I did it to save us, but I couldn't save my husband. He was dead before I took matters into my own hands. Will Allah forgive me?"

"Calm down Iman. Everything happens for a reason. Maybe that was a test for you and I know for sure if your intentions were pure Allah would always forgive you. Besides, you never did anything wrong. Saving yourself from some Mafioso is not a crime."

"How do you know that they were Mafia?"

"You said they kidnapped you and kept you for a week. I can tell they must be some kind of Mafia then?"

"Yes, drug Mafia. My husband smuggled some drugs with my luggage, but he didn't deliver. He said he was wrong, and he didn't want to get involved in such things. Mamma, why do I always have to suffer? Why?"

"Allah tests those He loves the most."

"When will my test be over?

"It is already. Isn't it? Alhamdullillah you're safe and you did manage to escape without anyone's knowledge. Look at the bright side, you could have been stuck there."

"Yes, that's true," whipping her tears away she sat up straight and said, "I had met an old lady the day they kidnapped us. She gave me her number. You know Mamma, when I called her she never asked why and helped me just like that. She even gave me a dress and a bag too, and she told her son to drop me off at the airport. I think I must thank Almighty Allah for that."

55

ADAM HAD seen her cry many times. Sitting by the falls, wiping off her tears, she would run inside as soon as he would reach her.

"I have seen her cry whenever I've caught her sitting by the falls. Why does she do that?" he asked Mamma.

"I am trying hard to console her, but her grief is much deeper."

"What's her problem, Mamma?"

"Nothing dear. She is just alone. What about you, do you want to read any more books? I was thinking if you like Mujahid would take you to some of our prominent Imam sahibs. They will surely answer all of your questions better than us."

"I think I am fine here. I am getting all my answers from the Qur'an and you guys are the best.

Besides, we would have to travel a lot. I mean, these Imams could be far away right?"

"Yes dear, if you say so."

56

FOR MAX the past six months had been a blessing. He had never imagined that a kid half his age would be such a wonderful friend. Who would guide him and help him plan his last job. His biggest hurdle was getting the information about that American, but for Dexter it was a no-brainer.

"Dublin said the man died years ago, but he has a son who lives in New York, some fancy Architect. You said you killed them both, didn't you?"

"I did, they gave me two life sentences."

"What did your conviction sentence say? Killing two lives or attempting murder?"

"I guess it's both, killing and attempting. I never noticed."

"Didn't your lawyer tell you?"

"I couldn't afford a private lawyer, and you

know how these district attorneys are. They won't talk much. Besides, mine was an open and shut case. I was guilty."

"How did it happen? I mean, didn't you plan well enough?"

"I did, but not well enough I guess. I still wonder who called the police. There was no one else in the house, and it was midnight. Plus I had cut the telephone lines. That house was too far away from any neighbours. If only they hadn't come right away, the kid would've died."

"Things happen and you learn from them."

"Can you tell him to find the kid's exact address?"

"He already did. He lives in a penthouse on Park Avenue, upper Manhattan. Do you want him to send a guy to follow him?"

"No. I guess it's okay. I'll do the rest myself. It'll cost me a fortune this way. I don't even know yet if they approved my request."

"You would be a lucky person if they did."

57

ADAM STOOD by the falls waiting for the driver who would take him to the Masjid, desperate to finally start the new chapter of his life. The more he learned about Islam, the more he got tied to it. Two days before that day, sitting by her sofa he had finally asked, *"Mamma, would you tell me the process to convert to Islam?"*

"Dear, for converting to Islam you need to recite the first kalimah, loud in front of at least two Muslims," she replied calmly.

"So, if I want to be a Muslim, I would simply have to recite that, that's it? Don't I have to go to the Masjid for it?"

"Now there isn't any obligation for that, but declaring your conversion in front of as many Muslims as you can is better, so I would suggest you visit the Masjid at the Raicot bridge."

"How did father do it? At home or Masjid?"

"Masjid dear. We have a huge Muslim community there.

They witnessed him convert."

"I would love to do that, Mamma."

"Do what?"

"Convert into Islam. For that, I would like to visit the Masjid as soon as possible."

"Alhamdullillah, my dear grandson. You've made me a happy granny today. I'll send Khadim to deliver the message to our driver. The day after tomorrow is a Friday. It would be best if you visited before Friday prayer. Come here, I want to hug you."

Adam smiled, remembering the emotional hug he had shared with his grandmother.

"The driver is here, Adam," Mujahid said.

"Good, let's go then."

58

"I AM so happy, Mamma. Did he really say that?" Iman was sitting by Mamma's lap in the library that evening.

"Yes, my dear. He said he's ready. He'll do anything to prove that the path his parents chose was the righteous one. So, they are visiting the Masjid today. He will recite the kalimah before Jummah prayer."

"Can't he just repeat the Kalimah here right in front of you and testify that there's no God but Allah, and Muhammad (peace be upon him) is His messenger? I don't think in Islam it's obligatory to go to a Masjid to accept Islam."

"Yes. You are right, but Adam wants to do it the exact way his father did. He wants to follow his footsteps."

"It must be really hard for him to forgive his father's actions. The way he raised him was miserable, even though he knew well what was right for Adam. I'm so relieved that he came out of those depressing thoughts. The thoughts he had started to build after he read his father's letter."

"You know, you were worrying about him more than me. I knew from the first day I met him that he would agree to what's right for him. He's such a nice boy, and his father did a great job raising him, a soft-hearted person as he is," Mamma added.

"Mamma, do you think I should go back? Ama has sent a message several times. She wanted me to live with her so badly. Isn't it bad that I didn't tell her anything? I am still confused. What should I tell her? The whole story?"

"No, my dear, I don't think you should tell your mother most of the things."

"What should I tell her, then?"

"I think you should tell everything but killing that man. You needn't have to tell her that; it could get her into misery as she is not that strong."

"You think I am strong? You know, until I told you, I used to have nightmares about Ahaan coming back to get revenge. I felt so light the moment I said it all."

"You'll feel even lighter when you tell all this to your mother."

"Yes, I think so too. I have an idea. Maybe I

should get ready and when the driver comes back from the Masjid I should go with him. That way, he won't have to come again."

"If you think you are ready to face the world, then it's a good idea, I guess."

59

THE SMALL prayer room at the Masjid was filled with men; even the outer veranda was occupied. Some men were sitting on the rug, waiting for the Khutbah, the sermon, and some were offering Nawafil. Adam stood near the Minber, the place from where the Imam leads the prayer and delivers his sermon as well. The Imam corrected his white cap and started his speech. "Assalamualaikum Wa Rahmatullahi Wa Barakaatu — before I start my usual Khutabah, I am privileged to announce that we have a guest here all the way from America. He is the grandson of a local resident from the other side of Chillas. Brother Adam is here with us for his testimony of faith; he is here to say his Shahada, Alhamdullillah. Let's not waste time and call Brother Adam, and as we will need a translator, for most of us don't understand his language, please welcome Mujahid Bhai who will translate Adam's speech."

"Thank you, Imam Sahib. I hope I addressed you correctly. I am truly happy to be here once again.

Only six months ago, I was standing right outside this window, silently observing the prayers. That was my first time ever to hear the Adhan and see you all pray from this close, and believe me, I was mesmerized. I am happy to announce that I am completely ready to submit myself to the will of God, as I have found the true purpose of life. And also, my happiness, tranquillity and inner peace lies in following the ways of Islam. Thank you."

Mujahid translated his speech with a broad smile on his face and said, "Imam Sahib, I guess it's time you let Adam recite the beautiful words."

"Adam, you may repeat whatever I say," Adam nodded, "I testify — La ilaha illa Allah, Mohammed Rasoolu Allah."

Adam repeated, then Mujahid translated the words in English for Adam, "I Testify that there is no god (deity) but God (Allah), and Mohammed is the messenger of God."

A sudden rush of applause filled the atmosphere; everyone greeted Adam with, "Mubarak." Hugging and congratulating him, some people threw garlands made with beautiful fresh flowers over his head.

After the Jummah prayer, all three of them stayed the night at the hotel, as they could not travel back the same day. The greetings and hugging continued till midnight; people from far away came to the hotel just to greet Adam and welcome him to the new world. Many offered dinner parties at their houses, but Adam told all of them to join him at the dining hall in the hotel. The dinner was exclusive as the hotel management served their special Pulao for everyone.

60

"ASSALAMUALAIKUM," SAID Adam as he entered the library.

"Wàlikumassallam, Alhamdulillah, my Grandson is a Muslim now. I hope you find peace following the Deen and never look back." Mamma hugged him and they sat side by side.

"I am already at peace, Mamma, but surely I will try my best to be firm and not lose my faith over worldly things."

"Mamma, the driver is ready and he is waiting for Iman Behan," Mujahid said, standing by the door.

"What? Is she leaving already?" Adam questioned.

"Yes Adam, she has to go back to her parents. Mujahid, you may knock on my bedroom door, and tell her that the driver is ready," Mamma said.

Before Mujahid turned around, the door to the

room opened. Iman came out with her bag and said, "I am ready."

She rushed inside the library, said her farewell to Mamma, and slowly turned around and whispered, "Assalamualaikum."

"Wàlikumassallam," whispered Adam in reply.

"Oh! Mamma, is she going because of me?" Adam said after he saw her rushed out of the fort with Mujahid carrying her bag.

"No dear, what made you think that? She was happy for you, it's just that she is now ready to face her world and tell them her story. She needs to tell her mother all that happened to her."

"Mamma, you never told me what really happened to her and why she was so upset to leave her city and come here? I am sure you know that, right?"

"Yes, I sure do but I cannot possibly tell you everything; it's not my story to tell. All I can tell you is that she has fought hard to get back to her country. Her husband was involved with some kind of Mafia men and they got kidnapped by them. She spent quite a lot of time in their captivity where her husband died and she was lucky enough to get out without the notice of law enforcement," Mamma replied.

"So, no one knows that she was there? How's that possible? Maybe they are looking for her?"

"The building caught on fire after she ran away, and she also received a call from the NYPD when she landed at the Islamabad airport inquiring about her husband's whereabouts. She told them that he gave her the ticket and her passport a week before the flight and didn't contact her since then. And then, after three months, they sent her a letter telling her that her husband had died due to a fire in a downtown building."

"Oh! This must be hard for her. I think she was brave for travelling alone after all that."

"She sure is,"

"Do you think she will be fine going back? She must have relatives who would ask a lot of questions about her story."

"Ah! She is stronger now; I hope she finds her a new match sooner rather than later who could heal her soul's wounds."

"Hmm." Adam didn't know what to reply, he hadn't had any clue about things as such. He had never thought about getting married himself.

"Is it mandatory for a Muslim to get married? If yes, then I really never thought about that before."

"No, getting married is one of the few things Allah and our prophet approve as a good deed, but they never said that it was mandatory. Yet, they have emphasized that the best way to live in this world is with one's spouse; this way, one can achieve many goals. For instance, they get far away from illegitimate relations, as having relations without marriage is one of the biggest sins in Islam. Also, they can produce offspring to serve Islam, and as a result, one gets loads of Sawaab, reward in Jannah. Getting married is considered as the most beautiful act of human race in Islam."

"Fair enough!"

61

THE MORNING was bright. Adam placed his coffee mug over the edge of the window. For the past month he had learned very little about Islam, only the basics. With Mamma being sick, he could not focus on anything else her. Even though he had begged her to let him take her to the hospital or at least let him bring the doctor there, but she refused his offers and insisted that they stay close to her and learn whatever she knew before she died. The past month was hard enough for all three of them, Adam longed for her to be in good health, to live a long life and to teach him, to guide him, and be there for him, but her condition got worse. Mujahid had never imagined any life without her.

"Mujahid, I — I want you to send I — Iman and h — her mother a message t — that I — I would love to see them before I go," Mamma said.

"Yes, Mamma, I've also requested Hakeem

Abdullah to come here and give you a check-up," Mujahid said while getting up, he left her room with a small nod to Adam who was standing by the large window.

Adam turned around and said, "You're not going anywhere Mamma, you'll live; you have to live for me!"

"D — dear Grandson — n come here s — sit near me," Mamma mumbled.

"Yes, Mamma, I am here," Adam took his place over by the side of her bed.

"I — I want — t you to understand w — what I am about to say is for your own betterment, not for Iman, not for me. Do you understand?"

"Yes, Mamma, I do."

"I want you to marry Iman. S — she has the power to keep you on the right path, love you, and provide you with a happy married life," Mamma said with a strong voice, stronger than Adam had ever heard her speak. Adam stood there, mouth shut, thunderstruck with her words.

"Are you even listening, A — adam?"

"Yes, Mamma, I am. Do you really want that? I don't think I am ready to get married. You know I don't want to repeat my father's mistake; I want to learn about Islam's practices first."

"This would be my last wish, grandson. I — I would've waited for you to say it for yourself, b — but under these circumstances, I think I won't be living any longer than a few days."

"Please, don't say that. You'll live," Adam said.

"Say I — in-sha-Allah."

"In-sha-Allah."

MUJAHID, YOU know I cannot marry her. This is insane, I know I became a Muslim and all, but I simply cannot get married yet, let alone marry her... it's impossible," Adam said while pacing to and fro in front of Mujahid in his room upstairs. After telling Mamma that he would think about it, he went straight to Mujahid, grabbed his wrist and dragged him upstairs to his room.

"Why is it impossible? What's wrong with her?"

"Nothing is wrong with her, it's me; I think I am not right for a girl like her – what if I end up like my father?"

"You won't, In-sha-Allah, because you are Adam, not David. Besides, she needs you more than you think. She has lost her husband and she would need a person who could take care of her, who could make her feel like a princess."

"Ah! That's the point; I am not that caring person you are describing."

"You are, you just don't know yet."

"Don't tell me who I am. I know better than anyone else who exactly I am," Adam shouted. Then he added with bitterness, "Besides, why don't you marry her. You're caring enough."

"You're forgetting Mamma's wish, and please, don't be mad. Listen, you need to give yourself a break, read The Quran and pray some Nawafil, and you'll find your answers," Mujahid said and left leaving Adam flustered.

63

“MAYBE, I’M the one who is wrong here. Maybe I need to deal with this in a fair way, but how?”

Adam whispered, while sitting on the Janamaz, which, a few months ago, was merely a six by three rectangular rug for him. Saying those beautiful words of kalimah led him to understand Islam in a way he had never imagined before. Then why was he being so stubborn in this matter?

“You need to start thinking with an open mind. I’m glad that you took my advice, though.”

Adam turned around and saw Mujahid standing by the door, leaning back to the wall with crossed hands, smiling calmly.

“How? How did you know that praying or reading The Qur’an would help me?” Adam said those words with the kind and intimate voice that revealed his soft side.

"Well, I just told you to do what I would do in such conditions, The Qur'an always soothes me and Namaz makes me realize there's a supreme being above us."

"I'm surprised, you're so calm and soft — you need such supports too?"

"Of course my dear I do. Well, a little less than you do, but there are times when I get frustrated too," Mujahid said with a soft smile.

"Why are you smiling like this?"

"I can see you're ready to become a groom?"

"Haha, very funny! Not yet, but I'll surely give it a thought now."

"You know, I grew up in an orphanage. Our headmaster over there used to say never think twice when deciding what seems best for you. Always be grateful for the little things that Allah offers you, despite the fact that they seem little, yet only Allah knows that these little gifts will turn out to be the greatest things that have ever happened to you. Besides, Iman Behan is a whole package of happiness. How could you even doubt it for a second?"

"What do you mean a whole package? She's just a girl."

"Ah! Her husband died right in front of her, and she has been in misery since then. I really don't know if Mamma has talked to her yet — maybe she is only requesting them to come here for this. If she agrees on marrying you, then I must say, she would be a strong woman, and believe me, a strong woman is always a blessing. Why do you hate her this much?"

"I don't hate her. In fact, I like the way she follows her rituals – you know, I first saw her in the plane; she was travelling back to Pakistan. Very bold and confident, yet I felt misery in her eyes. I don't know what I thought of first. Maybe it's the fact that I grew up thinking that marriage is the biggest hurdle between you and your success."

"So, it's a yes?"

"You are such a horrible person, you know that, right?" Adam threw a pillow at his face.

"Horrible or not, I did the job here, didn't I?"

"Well!"

"Don't well me, okay? I know you're popping happy popcorn inside the big tummy of yours." Mujahid threw back the pillow over Adam that landed on the edge of the bed.

"Big? Honestly? I'm a smart guy."

"Yeah, yeah. Smart yet not *smart*."

"Look who's talking."

"Okay, cut it out. You're being such a baby. Are you in or not, 'cause we don't have a lot of time here?"

"Why such a rush?"

"I need a yes before you start using that little brain of yours."

"My, my. I'm doomed, and stuck with the most

obnoxious wizard here who'd do his dark magic on me if I don't agree with him." Adam waved his hands dramatically and got up from the Janamaz, placing his Quran on Mujahid's chest. He walked past him and went straight to the library.

64

❝AS WE promised, this month we will be releasing those of you who have spent their sentence with good behaviour and who promise to behave like gentlemen for the rest of their lives. I hereby announce the court release of four of our senior prisoners, namely, Mr. Haxtun Roy, Mr. Naveed Akhtar, Mr. Samuel Box, and Mr. Maxwell Galati. I hope that all four of you will make us proud and become useful members of the world outside," the jailer said, and the other prisoners started cheering for the lucky ones.

"We will," whispered Max, who stood silently at the corner, away from all the hugging and wishing. For almost thirty years, he had served a sentence he didn't feel he deserved. All he did was to set them free from the hardships of their lives, yet all he got in return were the hardships he had never wished for. No matter how hard he tried to be the one who'd bring change in this world, to let the world acknowledge his efforts for a better world, they never understood.

They cursed him for bringing misery, although that was never his intention. His lord had given him a second chance, and all he had to do was to prove them wrong and show them that all his past actions were to bring happiness, not misery.

198

ADAM SMILED when his daily reminder beeped on his smart phone, and he glanced at the Hadith that popped up. It had been seven years since he had moved back to America; happily married with four kids and the most loving wife. Not at all a loser.

While waiting for his eldest son by the gate of the Islamic school, Adam went back to the times when Mamma used to teach him things about Islam.

"I still can't believe that I spent half of my life believing that marriage could ruin me," Adam whispered, "Thankfully, Mujahid had been there for me. I was an enemy of myself," Adam said out loud laughing at himself.

"Assalamualaikum, Baba Jan. Where's Aiman? She should be here by now." Hamza hopped in the front passenger seat.

"She went back to look for you. What took you so long?" Adam turned his attention towards his seven-year-old son.

"Actually, my art teacher told me to wait for her. She gave me some supplies for the poster I have to make for the class, you know."

"Ahan! What kind of poster?"

"I have to show the complete process of salah through drawings."

"Let's go Baba, he's nowhere to be found,"Aiman said while taking a seat at the back without even glancing up.

"You fool, I'm here already," Hamza said.

"Hamza, where were you? I looked for you everywhere."

"Aimy! He's your older brother, call him Bhaiya. How many times do I have to tell you?"

"No Baba, he's a baby."

"I'm not."

"Yes, you are."

"I'm not."

"Oh, cut it out okay, no one's a baby here. And recite the Dua for travelling."

With that, they all started reciting the Dua in their usual manner, together in a chorus.

"Glory to him who has subjected this (vehicle)

to us, and we could never have it. And verily, to our Lord we indeed are to return."

"Baba, when is uncle Mujahid coming?" Aiman inquired while getting out of the car.

"Oh, Aimy, Baba has told you a thousand times before that he's going to come tonight. Couldn't you be a little patient?" Hamza barged in before Adam could even open his mouth.

"I did not ask you," Aiman said with an annoyed look on her face.

"Assalamualaikum, little ones, how was your day today?" All three of them turned and saw Iman standing with open doors and a jug of orange juice in her hands. The twins emerged from behind her and grabbed Adam's legs.

"Baba, Baba."

"Assalamualaikum, lunch ready?" he asked his wife while taking the two angels inside with him.

"As always." Iman went into the kitchen and started serving their lunch.

"You two wash your hands first," ordered Adam.

"I wanted to get some groceries from the Pakistani store. You know I'm planning to prepare a traditional Hunzai dinner for Mujahid bhai. What do you say?" Iman started talking the moment they settled at the dining table.

"Perfect! He would love it as he has been away from his country for a long time now, but he's coming tonight. How would you manage to make the dinner so soon?" Adam said.

"I have prepared a few things for tonight, and I'll make the rest tomorrow night. By the way, did you ask him about what his plans are for marriage? Why is he not getting married?"

"Zillions of times, but he says he will, someday. I hope that day comes soon. Hey, why don't we force him to marry someone here, that way he'll be near at least?"

"You know he likes historical places."

"Yes, but he's been out exploring the world for more than five years now. At least it's time for a break."

"Let him come; I'm sure you'll find a way to talk through this matter with him. Don't worry, he'll listen. InshaAllah. In the meantime, I'm going to search for a cute bride for him."

"Oh! Don't start all the fuss already. Who knows, there could be someone he wants to marry already," Adam said while taking the crispy potatoes from her plate.

"No, no, you're not taking that. I love them. I was keeping them to eat at the end. Oh, you're such a..."

"Mama, Baba, don't fight for the food," Hamza said with the cutest tone that they both paused.

"Hey, you don't talk to your Mom and Dad like that," Adam said while obscuring his smile.

"Yeah, the same way you don't fight in front of your kids," replied Hamza.

"Oh, I'm feeling old. My son's a grown up now," Iman said and picked the fried potatoes from Hamza's plate.

"Hey, Mama. What was that?"

"It's called Badla in Urdu, since you're his next kin. Haha."

Adam didn't hear her words. He was busy looking at his beautiful wife. How time flew by. It seemed only yesterday that she was dull and silent. He still remembered her eyes filled with fear and remorse. She was a totally different person back then, reserved and self-restrained. Their marriage gave her the confidence Adam had never imagined seeing her with before. She had turned out to be an amazing person... full of life and full of surprises, yet soft and sensitive at moments.

"What are you looking at?" she inquired with a soft smile.

"Nothing. Just admiring your beauty."

"Seriously? It's been more than seven years. Most couples would start fighting by now. Besides, you should at least use a different phrase now."

"We won't fight."

"Why so?"

"Because I adore you, and you are my guru."

Iman just smiled a wider grin and got up from

the chair.

"So, will you take me to the Pakistani store today?" Iman asked when she returned with hot tea.

"What about kids?"

"We'll go with you. Please, please." Aiman bounced up and down.

"Well, okay, if you all behave and finish your homework before I'm back," Adam said as they settled down on the couch.

"You two go change your dresses and tuck yourselves in for a nap," Iman ordered the elders.

"Owe, why don't Ahmed and Amal get their naps?" Hamza moaned, kissed the twins and headed for the stairs.

"It seemed like yesterday when I last saw Mujahid at Mamma's funeral," sighed Adam.

"Although it's over seven years now, he hasn't even met any of our kids yet."

"Hmm... you did a great job letting them talk to him on Skype, though. It's been really good for their upbringing. Oh no, it's almost two o'clock. I should get going now. Just let the kids get ready for five o'clock. We'll go to the store as soon as I come back. Okay, Fè-Amanillah," Adam said and marched towards the door.

"We'll be ready then, Allah Hafiz."

Adam drove past the driveway and when he hit the road. He noticed a black sedan parked right by the main gate of his villa. A rental. In it he saw a grey-haired man he had never seen before. The man had a scar on the left side of his face. Adam glared at him for a while then drove away.

66LET'S GO, Mama. Baba's here,"Aiman was practically dragging her out.

"Oh Aiman, have patience. Your father has just arrived – he has to wash and change first. Assalamualaikum! Let me take this," Iman greeted her husband, taking his briefcase and coat.

"Baba, when are we going? I've done my homework, but Hamza here, he gave Mama a very strong time. He never listens to her," Aiman said in her own little style.

"She meant hard time," Iman whispered in his ears while Adam smiled.

"I did not. I've done my homework, Baba."

"That's very good. We'll be leaving soon after I've changed," Adam said and went straight into the bathroom.

In about an hour's time they were busy shopping at the store.

67

THE MAN with the scar was waiting for the right time. The long lost smile on his face had returned that day. He had been searching for the very person whose house lay right in front of him like a hungry dog sniffing its way towards food. Maxwell Galati knew he didn't have enough time to comply his plan, yet he started arranging things. With his grey hair and soft tender muscles, his job became more unwieldsome than he could ever have imagined.

"I have to do it for the sake of the world, to save humanity from slavery. I have to finish what I started. It won't be hard – the family always spends the weekend at home. No visitors. No rushing," Max said while he entered the house.

He had copied the front door key from Iman's set when she had accidentally left it in her car one day. Otherwise, it was impossible for him to enter as Adam had built a villa that was more like a fortress for his family in the suburb of Princeton, far from the busy world. There was a very large round open-air atrium at the centre of the house, connecting each and every room to it. The property had a beautiful garden with a pond in the centre and jogging tracks all over it. It could be accessed from the living room at the ground floor and the bedrooms up on the first floor through different sets of stairs. The outer wall had no windows, just one main entrance door; isolating the residents from the outer world.

Most of the bedrooms were far apart. The master bedroom was connected with a separate room for the twins on the northern side of the building. Other than that, the rest of the rooms were far away from each other. It was a perfect place to perform the drama he had planned for them. He was smiling with success after completing his tasks like hiding a remote-control bomb, a strong rope, and a duct tape in each room, and stashing all the weapons from the house. Overriding the alarm system surveillance system, and cutting the telephone lines. There was just one difference this time; he had to take care of their mobiles.

He settled himself under Hamza's bed with the dagger in his hands. Hiding his body beneath that bed was easy. It was a car-shaped bed that had big round wheels on all four sides. A splendid place in between them for hiding.

"All done, I just have to wait for the right time now," Max sighed while closing his eyes.

"OH MAMA, try this one, it tastes amazing," Aiman bounced up on her seat while they were having a great time with the ice cream session at the mall.

"Hey, mine is better than yours," Hamza barged in as always.

"Okay, you two don't start it over there. Every flavour has its own taste," Adam cooled the tempers before it could reach its peak.

"Do you wanna go home now?" Iman inquired in a soft tone.

"Mama, please! A little more fun," Hamza begged her.

"Hamza, it's getting late."

"But Baba, it's Saturday tomorrow."

"Yes, and you know we have to prepare things for

your uncle's visit. I need to get some rest after that. We'll be having fun all weekend," Iman explained, and they walked towards their car.

When they reached home, Adam, as usual, let everyone out and headed towards the garage to park his car.

"Mama, can I watch TV for an hour now? It's not a school night. Please?" Hamza said. As soon as they were inside the living area, he started jumping up and down.

"Only for fifteen minutes, until I get your bed ready for you," Iman said and climbed upstairs to the southern side of the house. She took the bed sheets out from the closet just by Hamza's bedroom door and went in.

69

MAX OPENED his eyes at the sound of the door. He could hear someone walking into the room. He tightened his muscles, trying not to make any sound.

"Ah, the smell, it's perfect. I can feel her - it's the wife." Max's heart was beating hard, "Oh, she's changing the sheets. What should I do now? Should I begin?"

She hummed while taking off the old sheets from the bed. Moving towards her left, her foot hit something.

"Ah, Hamza, if only you could put your toys back on the shelves," she said. Picking up his car, she turned towards the toy corner.

"Alas, she's going towards my bag with the bomb." Max turned sideways to find a way to see what was happening, but it was impossible for him to see beyond those huge, black, wooden tires.

"Maybe, it was a bad idea to hide under this stupid bed," he said to himself.

Then, he heard the door bang shut. Everything went silent again.

I MAN WENT downstairs to check on the twins who were playing in their ball house by the TV.

"Did you make their beds? I think they should be in bed by now," Adam said because he wanted to watch the news.

"Yes, I did. Hamza, get up, come with me. And you too, Aiman." They obeyed and followed her.

"Mama, what dessert are you making tomorrow?"Aiman inquired while climbing up the stairs.

"I'm making kheer. Remember the one you like a lot?"

"Oh, the white creamy one?"

"Yes, and it's not cream. It's rice powder with milk and sugar."

"Oh."

"Would you please go to your room and change into your pyjamas? They're by your bed."

"Okay,"Aiman moaned and crossed the hall towards her room.

"Hamza, go change your clothes and brush your teeth while I make her bed."

"Okay Mama. You're gonna come back to tuck me in, right?"

"Yes, I know you're a baby," Iman said, smiled and she left Hamza by his door.

"Mama, why isn't my room near yours, just like the babies?"

"Because, my dear, you are a grown up. When you were a baby, you used to sleep in that very room." Iman twinkled, yet she knew it was hard for the little angel to sleep in a separate room far away. She had argued a lot about the matter with Adam. In her community, people never let the little ones sleep alone. At least the siblings sleep together, but Adam was persistent, that in Islam, boys over seven years shouldn't sleep with their parents or sisters.

"Recite the Dua for sleeping," she reminded Aiman, and the Dua echoed with the glowing stars in her room. She waited for her to close her eyes. The moment Aiman was tucked into the bed she started snoring. Iman recited Ayat-ul-kursi in a humming tone, kissed her doll and slowly closed the door behind her.

"Hamza, get out of the bathroom." Iman knocked at the bathroom door in the hall.

"I'm out Mama," Hamza said and opened the door.

"So, ready baby?"

"Please don't call me a baby? I'm your eldest son, Mama."

"You sure are." They went inside his room.

"Mama, why can't I stay up to welcome Uncle Mujahid?"

"Because he is coming late at night, and you can meet him in the morning. Now close your eyes and sleep."

"Will Baba go to the airport right now?"

"Yes, he is leaving in a while. Now shush!" She tucked him in, repeated the same recital prayers, waited for him to close his eyes and went out, closing the door behind her.

71

NO MATTER how detailed his planning was or how precise his calculations were, unexpected things happened that always made him feel like the burning fire that doesn't seem to know where it will end. Max had to rethink his schedule and do it faster as well for he didn't expect any guests with the family. He had been watching them long enough to know that they had never strayed from their typical schedule. Especially on weekends, when it was always family time.

The clock echoed its chimes when Max came out of Hamza's room, satisfied with the job done. He went straight to his next room— the girl. With a swift move he opened the door and closed it behind him. Smiling.

❝IT'S ALMOST one o'clock, Adam. Where are you? Is the flight on time?" Iman said, as she tilted her neck to hold her mobile while pouring out a glass of juice.

"Yes, we're just twenty minutes away. Don't wait for us. I'll serve Mujahid myself. You get your sleep. Tomorrow we have a long day."

"Are you sure?"

"Yes dear, I'll be up with you in an hour or so."

"I have arranged things on the table, and I am going to bed now, Wàlikumassallam," she said and placed her mobile on the table.

IMAN WENT inside the twins' room to check if they were alright. She just listened to their sound breathing and saw them lying inside their beds, without turning on the lights, knowing that they might be woken up. She closed the door and went inside her room but before she could step any further towards her bed, she felt something hard on her head and fell to the ground.

When she opened her eyes again, her head hurt and she felt weight over her belly. When she tried to move her hands, she found them tied with a thick rope to the headboard of her bed. She turned and saw an old man with a scar on his face. She tried to shout but her mouth was duct-taped.

"Hello, you're up earlier than I thought you'd be. I am Max and you seem to be the wife. Pity I cannot let you talk. They are downstairs and we have to keep things quiet around here," he whispered. Iman started making vigorous movements trying to make some sounds, but before she could make any difference he came nearer and said, "Shhh, the kids are sleeping. Do want them to see how their parents died?" with that he placed a square piece of cloth over her nose.

"PLEASE HAVE a seat," Adam said, gesturing towards the dining chair.

"You're acting strange," Mujahid said.

"How strange?"

"You're being too formal, and this dinner it looks like you guys have an army to feed. It's me, remember? And I had my dinner on the flight."

"That's too bad. You should eat. Iman made all this just for you. You know her. Then again you've had your dinner?" Adam said.

"Man, I will eat but can't` promise to eat it all."

"That's okay."

"It's already too late. You can go right away and sleep. I'll find my way to the guest room. It's in the west wing right?"

"I'll go once you're all set. Besides, Iman must be

fast asleep right now, so no worries."

"Then join me. We have lots of things to catch up on."

"Like, where is your bride to be?"

"Or my wife, if you must know."

"You—you got married?"

"Not exactly, but yes I did. You could say that."

"What do you mean? Either you're married or you're not."

"It's a long story. I will tell you someday. In fact I have too many long stories to tell. You know, places I have been and the people I have met."

"Hell, I am dying to know. Each and every thing, but wait until you meet Hamza. He will get more stuff out of you, things that I could only imagine."

"He's such a fine boy."

"Just wait until he bombards you with a series of questions. He won't even give you any chance to answer them."

"And what about Aiman?"

"Oh, she is his boss. Come on, don't beat around the bush. Tell me about your wife or if she is your wife. You're giving me goosebumps."

"Nothing. Actually I don't know if she's alive or dead. I married her in Turkey and then lost contact."

"You mean you married her years ago, back in Turkey, say five or six years ago or you visited it recently that I don't know about yet?"

"Five years."

"You monster! How could you? And how could you say this so easily that you lost contact with her?"

"I told you it's a long story, and I will need your help to find her."

"Long or short, I am not going anywhere until I hear it."

"Adam," Mujahid said, gesturing towards the stairs.

"You are such a monster." Adam got up and said, "Let's go. I'll take you to your room, but get this straight into your head. I won't let you live until you tell me every single detail."

"Yes, boss."

WHEN ADAM reached his room, he saw the tiny strip of light coming from underneath the door.

"What's this? Oh, dear wife, I'm here. Let's sleep, okay?" Adam said while entering his room. Its two o'clock in the morning and all the lights are on? She must be really mad. He looked up and found his wife half-conscious on the bed, tied with rope and lots of duct tape. Horrified, he hurried towards her. There was something on her chest.

A bomb with red a light blinking. A remote-control bomb; on it he saw a note.

"If you want to save your family, come find me. You have ten minutes. The clock is ticking."

Adam searched his pockets for his mobile

remembering, he had left it downstairs.

He reached the landline... Dead. He rushed to the twins' room and found the babies tied up too with a bomb over their bed. He went near them with the intention to get rid of the bomb, but there was another note.

"Don't try to disarm it. If you did save these two, you'll surely lose the others. Be a good father and listen to me. Come find me. I'm waiting."

He sped towards the other side of the house and encountered another frightening site. The kids were tied up on their beds, unconscious with a bomb. The note read:

Tic Toc, Tic Toc... Less than 5 minutes now. Find me!

Adam ran as fast as he could in search of the very person who had the answers. He looked into each room upstairs then ran downstairs. Atrium empty. Guest room empty.

"Mujahid?"

No one replied.

"Mujahid?"

Still no reply.

The living room, empty, even the kitchen. Every single place empty. He tried the kitchen's phone, but it was dead too. As he turned towards the basement door something hard hit him over the head and everything became blurry.

HIS HEAD throbbed, he felt like his heart had suddenly stopped beating and all the blood had drained down to his toes. He tried to stand up and found himself tied to the iron rod of the back of the huge drawing easel. An awkward position with his hands and both of his feet tied with the rod in a way that he was forced to sit on his knees.

"Hello? Adam? Anyone?" Mujahid said.

He was in Adam's office in the basement, he remembered retiring to the guest room.

"How in the world did I end up here? Where is Adam? Where is everyone else? I hope everything is alright up there."

Mujahid twisted his back trying to see the rope that forced him to stay bound to the easel. It was a thick rope, thicker than any he had broken out of before. The iron rod was bolted into the ground.

He knew he had to hurry in figuring his way out. He knew whoever had done this to him would have worse plans for the people upstairs.

A SHARP PAIN hit him the moment he opened his eyes. He tried to reach the source, but he realized that he was tied to one of the pillars of the atrium. He could taste the salts of the blood in his mouth. The bright light coming from top of the atrium blinded him. He twitched his eyes twice to clear his vision. The first thing he saw was an old man sitting on the lawn chair just a few feet away. Wrinkles were prominent on his face. Then, he noticed the scar. He was the man with the scar. Why do I always wait for the disaster? Why didn't I take any action when I first saw this hideous man?

"It took you long enough. I have been waiting for this very moment for a long time now."

"What happened to my family? Tell me they are okay," Adam inquired in a possessive tone.

"They sure are. I gave the kids their breakfast. I'm not a beast, you know. But not your wife, she didn't get any breakfast. I'm sure she can live, at Least to the extent I want her to. And your friend, oh, that one was hard. I didn't even have any gift for him, so I did my best to serve him. After all, he is so dear to you."

"Who are you and what do you want from me and my family?"

"Ah, pity. Don't you know me? I'm your father's beloved friend Max. I'm sure he had told you about me. I was his best friend."

"What? No, that's not possible. You can't be him. He's in Scotland, in some prison."

"Yes, I was in Scotland. I came here after I was released. I searched two long years for you to finish what we had started. I thought, wouldn't that be fair to give you your Father's gift?" Max said.

"What are you talking about? What gift?"

"Didn't your father tell you that I was his childhood friend? We played together for a whole year. We used to talk about elders, and why they always forced their children to do things they thought were right. Ah, your mother—she was so dear to me when I was but a kid myself, and then she left me. She left me because her elders told her to. She was a perfect example of one. Her parents forced her to wear those covered dresses and also ordered her not to talk to any boys at the school." Max stood up, came closer, and looked straight into his eyes.

T HE ROOM echoed with the sound of an alarm. Mujahid turned his head towards its direction and saw three cell phones lying on the table. One of them was his.

He looked down to the bolts between his legs. The bolts that seemed tight, but Mujahid knew he had a strong jaw. So, he bent his head and started twisting the bolt. The rust on the bolt tasted like blood and sand.

"IT WAS not at all by force. She did it by her own will. She knew what was best for her," Adam said.

Max kept on staring him, "No, it's not." He turned red instantly and continued, "It's what they say to calm us down. There's nothing like God or whatever you call it. It's just humans making stupid rules and forcing other people to follow them."

"You are the same. You never changed. Didn't you learn something from your life?" Adam ignored the harshness and inquired softly.

"No, you're wrong. I've learned a lot. I've learned not to trust anyone, not even your best friends; they have a tendency to break your trust, to break promises."

"People say Muslims are terrorists," Adam said.

"I've met these so-called terrorists myself in the jail. The people they call terrorists don't believe in anything. They are people who have made their own rules. People like me. And you know what the worst part is? These so-called peacekeepers call us terrorists because we don't follow what they want us to follow. We are not Muslims. We are not Christians. We have our own beliefs and it's our right for people to leave us be. I believe there is no God. Why am I forced to act otherwise? It's my belief, just as you say. Women covering themselves are acting on their faith. Nobody forced them to do so. Then why we are forced to leave our beliefs?" Max turned around and took his seat again.

"How can this be? There must be someone who made this world. There should be a supreme being. We all are equal in this world. How can places this big can be created without a supreme being?" Adam tried to buy some more time.

"Don't waste my time. Here's the deal. You admit that there's no God or whatever you call it, all these rules are made by men, and that you'll never force your kids to do things you believe are right. Then, I'll put this remote right here on your table and leave this place. If you don't, then you know what will happen."

"I can surely promise you that I never will force my kids or my wife to follow any rules made by me or any person in this world."

"Also, admit that there is no God."

"I testify that there's no God but Allah," Adam

instantly said those words without even thinking for a minute.

"How could you? You know I can finish you and your family with just one click."

"ALLAH: there is no deity save Him, the Living, the Eternal One. Neither slumber nor sleep overtakes Him. To Him belong whatsoever is in the heavens and whatsoever is on the earth. Who can intercede with Him except by His permission? He knows all that is before them and all that is behind them. They can grasp only that part of His knowledge which He wills. His throne extends over the heavens and the earth, and their upholding does not weary Him. He is the Sublime, the Almighty One!" Adam calmly recited the verse from Quran.

"Seriously, you still think that your God can save you?"

"Those who deny God's signs and kill the prophets unjustly and kill those who enjoin justice, give them warning of a woeful punishment. Their deeds will come to nothing in this world as well as in the hereafter; they will have no supporters."

"This is insane. You utter a single word, and I'll press the button."

"That will kill you too." With those words, Adam saw what he was waiting for.

"Go to hell, I'm done with my life. After you, I don't have any purpose left to live for."

The moment Max finished his sentence, he

realized that Adam was staring behind him. Max turned around and found the guest standing by the pond. He stood up as fast as he could and held up the remote and said, "Stay where you are. Hands up in the air or I'll blow the place up."

"I'm here. My hands are up." Mujahid raised his bare hands and moved closer. Suddenly, with a swift movement, he kicked his hand which held the remote control which splashed into the pond. Then, he kicked another full blast to his left side. Max staggered down to the floor, astonished with the sudden action. Mujahid grabbed him with his left hand, punched his belly and again across his face, hard enough that the old guy's nose started bleeding. Mujahid grabbed the large marble vase without even looking. He twisted and winged it over his head. The blow made a thunderous sound. Maxwell Galati instantly fell down to the ground. Blood gushed. Within seconds, he was lying still.

"Where is everyone else?" Mujahid said and started undoing the rope.

"Hurry up! My family... my wife!" Words were coming out of Adam's mouth with a mixture of emotions; happiness and anxiety stumbled all together. With tears streaming, he ran past Mujahid and hurried upstairs.

"Mujahid, you have to help me. Check the kids. They are in their rooms at the southern side of the house, and please find any mobile. They must be here somewhere, and call 911," Adam called back.

"I already did," Mujahid said and walked towards the stairs to the kid's bedrooms.

Sirens whirled from afar.

****

D EAR MUJAHID;

If you are reading this letter, it means I'm already dead and you visited my lawyer.

I've kept you bond for a long time. Knowing that you love to explore the world, I'm leaving you the sole owner of the profits I earned from my Scotland investments.

I advise you to take my grant and explore the breathtaking world with your own eyes.

Yours,

Mamma.

-Meet Mujahid Again-

In

Kapadokya

Book One

A Mujahid Khan Thriller

When Mujahid reaches the land of Cappadocia, East Turkey, he never realised he would discover the long lost story of an alchemist who had hidden his precious formula of medicine inside an underground city not known to the world except the Father of the Church of Kayseri.
Along with his discoveries, he meets some friends, whom he cherishes with his heart, only to realize later that not all that glitters is gold.

ACKNOWLEDGEMENTS

First of All, I would like to thank Almighty Allah for giving me the strength and courage to write. The list will be long here, as this edition has gone through many phases. I would love to mention all by names, but spare me if I forget anyone who had helped me in writing this book. Hunger is not just a book. It's a teacher, a guide and way more than just a book to me.

At first I should mention my fellow writers who helped me polish my skills: Jae Hall, James Peters, Cindy Lord, Peggy Williams, Ma'am Samina Hashim Ali, Ateefah Sana ur Rab, Sydney Jones Champan, Hanzillah Siddique, Javeria Khalid and many more. My editor of the first edition, and fellow novelist, Brett W. Hicks who helped me go through the publication process. Zahra Akbar for being there whenever I needed her and for editing the recent edition. My proofreader, Jessica Fraser.

Last, but not least, my family. My husband, Hassan khan, who supported me, and without him all of this would be meaningless. My parents, sisters and brothers. My nieces and nephews who had been my proof-readers, beta readers and not to mention my thesauruses. In other words, I am one of the few privileged writers who have a family that love books and adores each and every word that I write.

ABOUT THE AUTHOR

Tanzeela k. Hassan is an emerging Pakistani novelist. After finishing her Postgraduate degree in Foods and Nutrition, with a baby in her hands, she's now a mother of four and currently a stay-at-home mother.

Art is in her blood. From her parents to her siblings, each and every being in her family excels in some kind of art. When she was asked about how she discovered her talent as a writer she replied, "My parents managed to take us on many expeditions across Pakistan, accompanied with a personal diary and a sketch book along with their advice to take notes and draw what we saw. They would always encourage us to write about our trip, saying that we should use all of our experiences to enhance our creativity."

Being a citizen of a third world country, she finds it her duty to let the world know about the positivity and beauty her native country possesses.

She is also the proud Lead Compiler of Thazbook's Anthology Journal, a yearly anthology that provides a creative outlet for the tween reader. This project is the product of her dreams... to provide better positive literature for generations to come.

OTHER BOOKS BY
TANZEELA K HASSAN

TEMOLI

Thazbook's Anthology Journal provides your tween (9-14-year old) a creative outlet. It is a blend of both a journal and an anthology. Where we give our respected readers lessons to learn creative writing along with a treasure trove of inspirational stories written by international authors. TAJ believes in fostering the young ones to enhance their ability to write by providing them with activities and writing prompts to pour out their version.

THE VARIANT

Living down in the valley with infected plants and waiting for her brothers to bring back food from up the cliff, has always made Ayman anxious. Her urge to go up there deepened when her brothers disappeared. Desperate to explore the world above and to look for her brothers. She sets up to the unknown world. The world they call, the Metazorric Dimension